The Flight

of the

Black Swan

The Flight

of the

Black Swan

A Bawdy Novella

Jean Roberta

Lethe Press
Maple Shade, New Jersey

Published in 2013 by Lethe Press, Inc.
118 Heritage Avenue • Maple Shade, NJ 08052-3018 USA
www.lethepressbooks.com • lethepress@aol.com
ISBN: 978-1-59021-417-6 / 1-59021-417-X
e-ISBN-: 978-1-59021-384-1 / 1-59021-384-X

This is a work of fiction. Names, characters, places, and
incidents are products of the author's imagination or are used
fictitiously.

Set in Minion, HenryMorganHand, and Mutlu.
Cover and interior design: Alex Jeffers.
Cover art: Ben Baldwin.

Cataloging-in-Publication Data available from the Library of
Congress.

FOR MY SPOUSE MIRTHA RIVERA,
WHO HAS NEVER STOPPED CHALLENGING
AN UNJUST STATUS QUO.

Acknowledgements

I would like to thank Steve Berman, publisher, for suggesting a pirate expedition and then for launching this ship: a work which doesn't fit perfectly into any one genre. The look of this novella, designed by Alex Jeffers, with cover art by Ben Baldwin, surpasses what I imagined when I was writing it.

I am grateful to my late parents for introducing me to the late-Victorian operettas of Gilbert and Sullivan in the form of a set of LP vinyl records and the occasional live performance, and for bringing me with them to England for my father's sabbatical year, 1973-74, when we visited Penzance and other pirate-worthy sites on the southwest coast. My father's experiences in the U.S. Navy in the Second World War, and his lifelong interest in sailing, seem more significant to me now that his running commentary has ended.

Victorian erotica in general has had an influence on this novella, and so has the historical novel *A High Wind in Jamaica* by Richard Hughes, originally published as *The Innocent Voyage* in 1929, reissued by New York Review Books Classics in 1999.

Other general influences include (in no particular order) the wit of Oscar Wilde, biographical non-fiction about the more-or-less discreet marriages of queer women and men before the advent of the "Gay Rights" movement in 1969, family stories about my great-grandmother who made costumes for the silent films of Warner Brothers in the 1920s, and the stunning talent of a bevy of local drag performers and clothing designers.

Contents

One

Cupid's Cruel Aim

ALMOST THE WORST THING THAT CAN happen to a young lady is to be loved by her parents.

Consider it: attentive mothers and fathers do all in their power to protect their daughters from risk and notoriety—in short, from every experience which gives savor to life. Fortunately, I approached the age of majority with my most exciting memories of childhood intact. They kept me from dying of ennui, especially after I lost my dearest friend.

I am Emily X, born on the island of Jamaica to English parents who placed me with my brothers and sisters on a ship bound for England when we were young. At length we arrived, of course, but not before being kidnapped (as the newspapers termed it—"waylaid" would be more accurate) by pirates.

If you have no knowledge of my history before the beginning of this narrative, please forgive me for closing the door on that chapter of my life. I prefer to begin a new acquaintance with no preconceptions on either side.

Suffice it to say that when I was restored to my Mama and Papa at age eleven, no effort was spared to give me a "normal" upbringing. My mother even tried to arrange for my presentation at Court when I would be of age. She went into contortions to show me the proper way to curtsey to the Queen, and I was to be outfitted with three feathers for my head like a horse in a procession.

Pity the fate of a well-bred daughter! I would as soon be sold at an actual slave auction in America than to be displayed to all of Society.

What of marriage? I hear you ask. Dear Reader, it was never my goal. As things turned out, however—well, read on and you shall see.

MY MAMA WAS ALWAYS EXCLAIMING OVER my silken brown hair, my eyes as blue as the sky, my rosy coloring and the gentle curves of my figure. She seemed intent on assuring me that my physical beauty, at least, had not been spoilt by anything which might have happened to me earlier. I was no more capable of explaining myself to my parents than if they had been ancient Picts with no knowledge of English.

Lucy, my dearest friend at school, was a lively girl who understood me better. Yet even she believed that I carried unspeakable knowledge like hidden treasure under my clothes.

I learnt this one day when we were both fourteen, as I watched her aim an arrow at a target. She had been rehearsing for a school play, and she still wore her costume, which consisted of stockings, a man's white shirt and feathered wings attached to her back with straps. Her flair for drama was never confined to the stage. As she drew one strong, flexible arm back to give the arrow speed, I felt as if she were aiming it at my heart.

The school archery range was deserted except for us. After looking around quickly to make sure she wouldn't be overhead, Lucy spoke to me. "Emily," she told me in a low voice. "I don't care what those dreadful men did to you. They didn't steal your spirit. I hope you never marry because you're too good for a man, and I want you all to myself. Am I horribly selfish?"

"Yes," I whispered back. "You're not a proper lady, and I'm glad." She let her arrow fly, but turned her head to throw me a quick glance, and it pulled her trajectory to the left.

I felt absurdly proud that I could distract her so much. "Focus on what you're doing, Lucy," I told her, trying to sound like a schoolmistress. "We must go away together after graduation. We might have to become hunters and trappers in the wilderness, beyond the laws of civilization."

She laughed loudly. "I doubt that, dearest! I only need to wait patiently until I'm twenty-one, when I may do as I please." She switched her attention to her target, released another arrow, and watched it land quivering in the center. "Whoo-oop!" she shouted.

THAT NIGHT, I CREPT INTO HER BED WHEN all the lights were out, and eased myself under the bedclothes. She pretended to be asleep until I wrapped her in my arms and kissed her on the lips. She couldn't maintain her façade, and burst into giggles. Her hips moved beneath me.

"Ssh!" I told her, fearing discovery.

"Our nightgowns are in the way," she whispered. "Move a little so we can take them off."

When we were both naked, we admired each other as best we could in the dim light from the nearest window. Lucy grabbed both my hands and brought them to her exuberant, womanly breasts. "Emily, I want you to have me," she whispered as urgently as she could, holding the counterpane over us to muffle the sound. "I want you to do whatever you like. We can both be fallen women together. We'll have our own code of honor, no matter who scorns us."

She reached beneath the mattress to bring out the candle she had hidden there. I had no doubt that she had already experimented with it alone. I was equally sure that she believed a real loss of virginity must be a two-person undertaking.

Dear Reader, the pleasures of Venus are too thrilling to be covered by a blanket of silence. Surely you knew when

The
Flight
of the
Black
Swan

you embarked on my story that it would prove thoroughly candid.

I didn't know what to say, so I wrapped my arms about Lucy and gently pressed my lips to hers. For a long while, we kissed like bosom friends. Then she pushed her tongue in between my lips and my teeth, and the intrusion gave me the strangest feeling between my legs, as though she were tickling me there.

She withdrew from me to see my expression. "That's a French lover's kiss," she whispered. "It's in Mademoiselle Rosier's French book about the arts of love."

"Did she lend it to you?" I could hardly believe it.

Lucy laughed. "No, silly," she answered. "I can unlock doors without a key. I'll show you later. Do it to me now, Emmy."

She wanted to be unlocked, invaded, burgled and read from her head to her toes. I wanted to do every intimate thing described in the filthiest of French books, but I didn't want her to think I lacked finesse. I decided to proceed cautiously, by degrees.

I caressed her breasts and felt the weight of them in my two hands. I nuzzled my face between them, enjoying the sound of her sighs. The tender buds that crowned her bubbies grew hard beneath my fingers. Feeling her beneath me was the sweetest experience imaginable.

Like a flower, she had her own distinct fragrance, which grew stronger as I nuzzled her neck with my lips and left a trail of kisses from her collarbone to her breasts to her waist and the soft skin of her belly. I could hear her breathing as I nudged her thighs apart and enjoyed the aroma of the dark curly hair between them. On impulse, I kissed her hairy cleft. When she squirmed, I imagined that her cunny was an animal with a mind of its own.

"Emily darling," she whispered. "Use your fingers. I want you to."

I slid an index finger into the sucking wet heat of her, and stroked her inner folds. She was like an oyster inside. I had touched myself there when I was sure no one would discover me, but discovering Lucy's inner sanctum was like exploring a new continent.

"Em!" she urged me. "Don't be afraid." She seized my hand and showed me how she wanted to be ravished. "I'll tell you if it hurts."

And so I sneaked a second finger in beside the first, and played her like a violin while she moved her hips in response. I found a little button of flesh inside her lower lips that grew hard when I touched it, so I teased it unmercifully. Lucy shivered violently, but didn't ask me to stop.

"Use the candle, darling," she told me, sotto voce. "You can pretend you're a pirate and I'm your captive."

"Pirates don't—" I began, but I had only had a very particular experience with them, and was hardly an expert on the whole salty tribe. I supposed that real defilement by criminals would be altogether less enchanting than Lucy seemed to imagine, but I wanted to fulfill her utmost fantasy.

"Don't scream," I threatened, making sure to growl as quietly as possible. "No one will save you, my girl. I have you now." And so I pushed the bigger end of the candle into her very wet opening, watching her closely to decide how to proceed. She clasped me with her arms and legs, urging me on with the most delicious of bounces and shimmies. I marveled at how much of the candle she could accommodate.

I lay on her belly, wrapt in her heat, feeling the rhythm of her beating heart as the increasing force of her breath stirred my hair. Knowing her this way made me realize how much more I wanted to learn about her.

"Oh!" she moaned when her crisis came. "I—love—you!" I withdrew my waxy love-spear one inch at a time, and felt it slippery with her juice. I had no way to tell whether I had made her bleed, but if I had, I hoped she was glad of it. What was done could not be undone.

"My love," she whispered, her breath tickling my ear, "that was the best! You'll see." She reached between my legs, but I seized her hand and held it.

"What're you doing?" demanded an accusing voice from another bed. There were shiftings and heavings in the beds around us, like the beginnings of an earthquake. I was afraid of a full-scale eruption that would leave us as shelterless as a real cataclysm.

"Nothing," I answered the accuser. I pulled Lucy back down under the bedclothes. "I'll come back tomorrow," I whispered in her ear. I pulled on my nightgown as well as possible, and slid out of bed as silently as I could.

THE FOLLOWING NIGHT, I SLIPPED INTO HER bed at the same time as before. This time, Lucy declared the game. "Emily," she promised, stroking my hair, "I intend to drive you mad with pleasure so you will never want anyone but me."

"I won't," I swore too loudly. I sensed that we were surrounded by listening ears, so I was afraid to say more. I forced myself to remain silent when she cupped one of my small, alert breasts in one hand and lowered her head to the other. Her hot, wet mouth on my nipple almost caused me to jump out of her arms. "Shh," she whispered.

The touch of her cunning fingers was almost more than I could bear, but the torment was sweet. I spread my legs to give her full access, not wanting to deny her anything. She kissed my little button before easing one finger into my opening, and I was relieved to feel pleasure, not pain.

"Lucy," I blurted. "Please be gentle. I don't want the candle. Not yet."

"Ssh," she whispered. "Don't worry." She kissed my belly and squeezed one of my arse-cheeks as she patiently frigged me with one finger. I became so excited that I soaked the sheet beneath me, and Lucy used two fingers to stretch me inside.

I moaned when I felt a burning deep in my center, and guessed that my maidenhood was gone. I didn't want Lucy to stop, and encouraged her to stroke me until I felt as if I were sneezing hard in my cunny. At length, she slid up to kiss my mouth, and we held each other as tightly as could be. "I'll never love anyone else, Lucy," I promised her. "I swear."

"Perverts!" came an uncouth voice in the darkness. "If you don't stop, I'll tell Headmistress."

I sneaked back to my own bed, as before, hoping that neither Lucy nor I would be expelled. I wasn't ashamed, even though I was now nearly as ruined as all my family and friends believed me to be.

SCHOOL WAS TRANSFORMED FOR ME FROM then until our final year. Even the most routine task or lesson had a pinch of fairy-dust in it because Lucy and I could do it together, or because it was part of the life we shared. She helped me improve at archery. In turn, my aim and concentration helped me to improve at fencing. Riding became almost unbearably sensuous. I could imagine Lucy and me as front-line warriors in an Amazon army.

AND THEN CAME DISASTER. AS OUR GRADU-ation approached, I asked her where we ought to settle when we had the means to live independently.

"You know what my parents are like, Emily," she answered. My heart immediately filled with pain like a broken boat filling up with filthy water. I could anticipate the rest.

"You have a suitor," I guessed aloud. "Someone they introduced to you. And they'll cut you off without a *sou* if you defy them."

"You're very clever, Emily," she admitted. "It will only be until my twenty-first birthday, and then I can do whatever I like."

By then she would probably be married, or at least engaged. Our dreams for our future had been truly scuttled. I didn't want to live in false hope, and I wanted her to feel some of the pain she had given me.

"I wish you joy, Lucy," I snapped. "I'm planning to go abroad, and I doubt if I'll ever come back." Little did I know at that time how closely my life would follow that careless pronouncement.

A Spinster and a Web

AS THOUGH THE FATE OF THE NATION WERE entwined with my own, our Queen lost her husband, Prince Albert, just before Christmastime. Her Majesty had the sympathy of all her subjects to comfort her in her grief, whilst I grieved alone for my lost love. One bright spot in the general gloom was that my mother gave up hope of seeing me presented at Court during the royal year of mourning.

I was a spinster in my parents' house, and I felt like a prisoner. The life of a governess might have been more tolerable, but the sort of father who would hire a woman with my reputation would have an intention other than the education of his children.

How I missed Lucy's kisses, the sure touch of her fingers, and the heat of her eager body! To keep myself from going mad, I began writing a story about a tribe of fierce women warriors inhabiting their own tropical island where palm groves sheltered them from the glaring sun and the eyes of strangers—although no one on the island was really a stranger to anyone else. Still, when two women wished to become better acquainted, it was best for them to find a special place where they could do everything they both desired, safe from interference by jealous rivals.

THE QUEEN OF THE ISLAND WAS A TALL, strong woman with flowing red hair. She looked like the picture of Queen Boudicca of the Iceni in an illustrated history of the British Isles that was given to me by my aunt for Christmas. In the book, the tribal queen sat proudly astride a horse, looking at the viewer as though at her army on the brink of battle. In my story, I (the narrator, Emilia the Bard) rode behind her, my arms clasped about her waist as we galloped over hills and valleys with the wind in our hair. I could feel the heat of her buttocks against my thighs and my cunny, and the rhythm of our horse was as captivating as a lively dance.

The queen knew the ride was stirring me to a lather, and she was as moved as I was. As her fragrant hair brushed across my face, I knew she wanted me to kiss her, to hold her in my arms as she held me in hers, to free her large, bouncing breasts from their leather jerkin and expose the curly hair in her trousers. However, she was entitled to take me first, and so as we rode, I resolved to remove all my clothes as soon as we had arrived at the appointed place. Of course, we wore no corsets.

WHILE WRITING ALONE IN MY BOUDOIR, IT was hard for me to complete each chapter of my story without setting the paper aside to raise my own skirts and seek out my overheated center. Touching myself, I was always amazed at how wet I had become. Sometimes I teased myself by squeezing my nipples through my bodice before sliding my pen between my lower lips, twirling it about experimentally, and then ravishing myself thoroughly with my fingers.

In the unlikely event that I should ever meet a warrior queen with a taste for female lieutenants, she would find me as loyal and willing as any. I would never desert her, and if she were a just ruler, she would value my devotion.

How I longed to cool my heated flesh in a bathing hole on the carefree island I remember as my first home, so far from

the gray skies of England! But I had to comfort myself with
such pleasures as were available to me.

ON A SUNDAY, AFTER CHURCH AND BEFORE
tea, I was allowed to spend an afternoon at Speakers' Corner.
This outing became the pinnacle of my week.

Joining the crowd in Hyde Park, I was forced to push past
other ladies with skirts as sweeping as mine. Due to the dic-
tates of fashion, women in public places made up in volume
what we lacked in influence.

A young man with the unkempt appearance and burning
eyes of a fanatic addressed the crowd. "Are we Christians?"
he asked in a ringing voice. "Have we no sympathy for the
wretched creatures who are still sold like cattle in America?
We have banished that evil from our Empire. Will we prosti-
tute ourselves by offering friendship to a new nation that fills
its coffers from the trade in human flesh?"

Slavery, I thought. The Americans were at war over it since
the owners of the great plantations had formed their own
Confederacy. By the latest accounts, their army was win-
ning.

I remembered the old plantation houses of Jamaica and the
great vats where sugar was turned into rum before Emanci-
pation. Most such signs of imperial grandeur had been over-
run by the plant life of the island before I was born. Once I
had gone exploring alone and walked into a ramshackle vil-
lage entirely inhabited by Negroes, where the youngest had
never seen anyone like me. A dark child no bigger than I had
offered me a bouquet of flowers.

At the time, I wondered whether the gracious young miss
had been taught to read and do sums like me. I could not
imagine that she and all her friends and relations could ever
have been owned like farm animals. When I came to understand the miserable status of slaves, it made me feel ill.

Efforts were made to enlighten me. When a pompous
young man, brother of one of my classmates, explained to

me in an insinuating tone that the control of primitive types by their betters was in their best interests, I could no more accept it than I could swallow vinegar.

In the present, a swaggering dandy brushed against me. "Pardon me, Miss," he said in a falsely conciliatory tone. A wide-brimmed hat shaded his face, making his expression hard to interpret. "Freedom for the oppressed is such a stirring concept, don't you think?"

As I tried to move away, I felt his hand on my purse, which he was trying to steal. "Stop, thief!" I shouted. In the ensuing commotion, he released my property and tried to find an opening in the throng. Looking back at me, he seemed startled.

"I meant no harm, miss!" he protested. "Please forgive me! Are you not—?"

"You're mistaken, man," I told him, and turned to leave.

He blocked my way, and I saw how tall and well-formed he was. He wore a tight waistcoat and a lace jabot under a sack coat, all slightly dirty and threadbare. The dark eyes under his hat glowed like coals. "I don't think so," he said softly. "I wouldn't forget such a handsome face, even though you were a child when—well, we won't speak of that. I would be greatly honored if you would accompany me to a place where we may converse privately."

"I'm not the sort of woman you take me for," I spat at him. *You can't imagine what sort I am,* I thought. I tried to take my leave, but the crush of bodies prevented me from striding away.

"And I'm not the sort of man you take me for," he responded *sotto voce.* "Trust me, Emily, if I may address you so. We have more in common than you can imagine on such an unfortunate first impression. Please let me take you to luncheon, and I will explain it all. I am John Greenleaf, and my friend here is James Featherlight." A plump, blond, pink-cheeked youth bowed shyly. He too wore a hat with a brim that shaded his face.

Our little group was attracting attention. "You may call us John and James," my new acquaintance continued. "Madam, we are most excellent friends, the bosomest of companions." He spoke rapidly, leaning as close to me as he dared. "I would sooner be hanged than to offer you any insult, if you take my meaning."

"Miss," said a large, red-faced fellow, "is this man annoying you?"

"Not at all," I replied on impulse. "He is my brother's friend, and we are just going to luncheon."

My two companions hired a carriage to take us to a poorer part of London, where the houses smelt of boiled cabbage and human waste, and urchins in rags stared at us openly. John led us to a humble shop which served tea and other items which I declined to smell, let alone to taste.

"Please excuse the surroundings, Emily," John beseeched me. "We can't afford to be seen. I'm so sorry not to have met you earlier, especially now that we have planned our departure. Your case has always moved me. Please forgive my presumption, but I feel as if we are kindred spirits. Ought I to know your brother if we cross paths?"

It was my turn to apologize. "Never fear," I assured him. "My brother John went to his reward many years ago. I claimed you as his friend because you share his name."

The man leant across the table, and spoke almost inaudibly. "I'm sorry for your loss, Emily, but my name isn't really John."

"And mine isn't James," added the other man.

"Softly," warned the man called John. "You must know that we are hunted men, dear. We served in Her Majesty's Navy, but a moment's indiscretion could have cost us our lives. We are fugitives, and we set sail for the Bahamas in three days."

"Did your indiscretion involve taking what didn't belong to you?" I asked.

"It does belong—" retorted "John" until he looked at his companion.

The one who called himself James reddened like a quickly ripening tomato. "Please forgive us," he begged. "We didn't mean to rob you. Well, we did, but only because we are in need. We could be hanged for unnatural vices."

"I see." I had never really been in doubt about their nature, but I hadn't considered the danger it placed them in.

The tea arrived. It tasted safe enough to drink.

"My sister Lucy hasn't forgotten you," said "John."

I had tried to forget her, with the same lack of success. I was instantly on the brink of tears. To control my feelings, I pressed a fist to my heart. "How is she?" I asked.

"Resigned to her fate," he answered. "Emily, I must speak frankly for your own sake. We would be proud to be your friends, and you haven't many."

"So I've noticed," I told him. "Was Lucy ordered to cut me dead?"

"I'm afraid so," said "James." "We're so sorry, Emily. Hottentots could learn savagery from those in Society."

Silence reigned for a moment. "You have no reason to trust us," he continued gently, "except that you have no better choice."

There had never been a possibility of my being presented to the Queen, and her grief had nothing to do with me. I could see that now.

"We sail in less than a week. We have a ship, a crew and a mission," said "John," as though thinking aloud. "Emily, can you sew?"

"Every woman can sew," I retorted. "I'm also a fair shot with a bow and arrow, and I can handle a foil, or, um, a sword. What are you really asking me?"

There were other customers in the shop, and "John" was aware of the cost of indiscretion. He came so close to me that for a moment, I expected him to kiss me. "You could be useful on our ship, the *Black Swan*, and we would see that you come to no harm. You probably wouldn't even need our protection, dear, because we all belong to the Green Men's

Society. We come from every ship in the Navy, and we all share a certain persuasion. Do you understand?"

"Perfectly." My heart felt full as I realized what I was being offered: a second chance at life with fellow-outcasts. Then I remembered my mother and father. "But my parents wouldn't! And if I sneak out of their house without a word, they'll think I've been kidnapped and murdered again. This time, it would kill them."

"James" looked down at the stained tablecloth as "John" gazed into space. "Would they accept your departure on your honeymoon?" he asked at last. "What if you were married to the son of a baronet?"

I stared, hardly able to believe what he was suggesting.

"It would have to be arranged quickly," "John" went on, "but I know a vicar who would do the deed as a favor to me as long as he can be kept out of the public eye. Green Men are everywhere. Emily, if you can play the role of a wife as required, you could help me to make peace with my father and gain my inheritance, if all else fails. The arrangement would benefit us both."

"I hardly know what to say," I stammered. "'James,' could you bear it?"

"Thank you for asking, Emily," he responded quietly. "If you and 'John' can bear it, so can I."

I reached across the table to offer "John" my hand in every sense. "You are a generous man. Shall I be known as Lady Tingley-Jones?"

"Shh!" replied my suitor. "Our names must be a sacred mystery until we are both safely on deck."

"What curious terms," I said. "I accept them, Sir, if your offer still stands."

Curious terms indeed. Had I not been desperate enough to run away to sea alone in a rowboat just to escape from confinement in my parents' home, I would have questioned my suitor more closely. Would he expect me to be his wife in every sense? At the very least, I would probably have to share a bedchamber with him and allow him to see me *en desha-bille.* And "James" might be watching from the wardrobe!

"John" looked genuinely happy. "Then our business here is concluded," he answered. He glanced at the local residents who were staring at us without shame. He paid the proprietor and led the way out of the shop as "James" brought up the rear. I was sure that such a position came naturally to him.

Outdoors, I asked "John" not to escort me home. "But I must be sure of your safe return," he protested.

"Then take me to the street where I live," I pleaded, "and watch until I'm safely indoors, 'John.'" Please understand that I can't introduce you to my parents or my siblings. I shall have to tell them everything in a letter to be read after I'm gone." In the carriage that brought us back to a modestly respectable neighborhood, we made our plans.

Three

Return to the Sea

I WAS USED TO KEEPING TO MYSELF, SO FOR the following three days, my family didn't seem to find me unusually reclusive. As the hours dragged by, my heart ached even as I longed to breathe salt air again. I composed the following letter:

Dearest Mama and Papa,

I hope it shall please you to learn that I have accepted a proposal of marriage from Mr. John Greenleaf, a former Officer in the Royal Navy. Please forgive me for answering him so quickly, but a higher Principle is involved. Mr. Greenleaf holds sacred the Free Will of all God's creatures, whatever they are called. He has arranged passage on a ship to America to fight in the War against Slavery in the Southern States. I have agreed to accompany him. Please try not to worry about me. I shall write to you again as soon as I am able.

Your loving Daughter,
Emily.

P.S. Please share this news with the younger ones.

I copied this out in a clear hand and placed it in an envelope that I left on my pillow. I packed a satchel that I thought my family could spare. Not a single gown, corset, hoop, petticoat or bonnet could fit into my baggage, and I had no desire to wear such garments on board a ship.

SHORTLY BEFORE MIDNIGHT, I SLIPPED OUT
of my parents' house, dressed in a pair of trousers and a shirt
that I had made for myself, covered by an old frock coat and
a hat of my father's with my hair tucked underneath. I hoped
that passersby would mistake me for a young man.

I arrived at the harbor for my rendezvous with my two new
friends. I felt very small in the shadows of tall masts, lit by
moonlight. A familiar baritone voice lilted in the darkness:

The sea runs bt yb in the west, Nellie,
And the wind is cold and keen.
True lovers all are blest, Nellie,
So keep your nt gbt gown clean.

The ditty was "John's" signal to me. I walked quickly in the
direction of his voice.

The *Black Swan* was a gallant three-masted wooden frig-
ate, rocking gently at anchor like a debutante waiting to be
presented to Mother Ocean. "John" had told me that it was
in ordinary, waiting to be called into active service as the
Navy outfitted warlike ironclad ships propelled by steam en-
gines. He surmised that our chosen vessel was scheduled for
retirement, and would therefore be considered less worthy of
pursuit than a more valued ship.

"Emily?" asked my fiancé. "How curious you look. But how
wonderful to see you." He turned aside from me to avoid
bursting into laughter.

"Laugh if you like, man" I answered. "Did you expect me to
arrive in full rigging, with petticoats as wide as sails?"

The man gave me a kiss on the cheek and a proprietary
hug. "But darling, we are to be married directly. Didn't you
think—well, appearance is an illusion after all. I defer to your
practical mind."

"James" approached as though unsure of whether I was
the same woman he had met in Hyde Park. "Emily?!" he
exclaimed. He looked at the division between my trouser

legs, and turned tomato-red, as was his wont. "I say, this is really—you look like a lad!"

"I'm dressed to travel with men!" I told him.

"But we were relying on you to—" he stammered. "Of course you're right, dear, you must dress for comfort and not for style. Welcome to our good ship, Emily."

I noticed dozens of men loading supplies onto the ship. These were the Green Men, the ones who were everywhere denounced as unnatural, and yet they looked as capable a crew as could be found. Some revealed themselves by the flamboyance of their gestures while discussing the disposition of stores meant for a long voyage, some by the sweetness of their voices, while some appeared as masculine as boxing champions.

Any magistrate in the city would condemn them all to the gallows! Words could hardly express my emotions as I saw them to be, in the words of the old song, "alive, alive-o."

"We must christen our good ship," said "John," "and exchange our vows, and set sail without further delay."

Lanterns swinging in the hands of the men fitfully illuminated various parts of the ship's deck and hull. I looked for her name and saw it painted on her side more crudely than seemed to befit a ship of the Queen's Navy. Her figurehead, a long-necked swan that gleamed black in the light reflected from the water, appeared as smooth as onyx. The ship, like its human cargo, was intended to escape detection.

"James" followed my gaze, and offered me his arm. "Emily dear," he began, "have you ever observed the grace of a swan's progress? And have you considered the impression made by any creature set apart from its fellows? That is how we think of our ship. She's like a black swan, proud of the natural plumage that distinguishes her from her snow-white sisters. Like us, she prefers the cloak of darkness."

"Then she is well-named," I remarked.

"John" linked his arm in my free one, and the two men escorted me on board. The men of the crew were passing boxes and barrels from hand to hand into the hold.

"Emily," said my fiancé, "Presently I shall introduce you to my crew. Now you must meet the vicar who is to marry us. Mr. Brown!"

A thin, solemn-looking man approached. "May I offer my best wishes, Miss," he said, extending his hand to me whilst trying not to stare.

"Thank you," I answered. I hoped he wouldn't wish me and "John" a large family.

WHEN ALL THE SUPPLIES WERE LOADED ONTO the ship, the men gathered with us on the deck of the fo'csle. I counted fifty, give or take a few. I saw ragged coats and patched trousers on boys and on gray-bearded men. In every face, I saw the light of hope. A ripple spread through the crowd as each man noticed me; I seemed to attract all eyes. "John" took my hand.

"Dearly Beloved, we are gathered here—" began Mr. Brown. And thus began the ceremony that would unite me in a covenant that was supposedly blessed by God with a man I barely knew. When Mr. Brown recited the phrase "forsaking all others," I glanced sharply at my bridegroom. I couldn't honestly promise that! "John" held my hand tightly, as though to assure me that we could be true to each other in our own way. Named as Sir Roger Tingley-Jones, my bridegroom made his vows to me and to God with calm affection. I repeated the words and silently promised him what loyalty I could.

And this is how I changed my status. I so wished that Roger could serve as proxy for his sister Lucy, and that I could marry her instead.

"Please excuse me," Mr. Brown muttered nervously, "I must take my leave at once." Two men of the crew followed him to the gangplank, as though to ensure that he would leave the ship as quickly as possible. Then pandemonium erupted.

The men on deck all shouted threats (in which "bugger" figured prominently) and gestured angrily at the half dozen men in naval uniforms who stood on the dock. Their uniforms were accompanied by gleaming bayonets.

"Peace!" screamed Mr. Brown, running with his hands in the air. "I'm a man of the cloth!" The men on deck swiftly withdrew the gangplank, and a shouted dialogue ensued. I felt as though I were watching a play.

NAVAL OFFICER: "Who commands this ship and what is her purpose?"

ROGER: "Mr. John Greenleaf, captain of a merchantman."

OFFICER: "Disembark, sir, by order of Admiral Bilge of the Royal Navy."

ROGER: "I find that unnecessary." (*With the co-ordination of dancers, the men of the crew hauled up the anchor and began setting the sails.*)

OFFICER: "Sir! You are charged with several capital offenses. Have you a Miss Emily _____ on board?"

ROGER: "No, sir. There is no petticoat on this ship. That would be unlucky."

OFFICER: "Sir! If you refuse to obey, I am entitled to shoot you on sight."

ROGER: "Oh, sir, I'm sure such rudeness is a disgrace to your upbringing. I must bid you adieu until we meet again in warmer surroundings."

The men on the dock fired several shots, but by this time, their assault accomplished nothing except a tear in one of the jibs.

The men on the ship cheered, hooted and whistled as the ship moved serenely into deep water, picking up speed as the wind filled her sails.

I couldn't imagine anything more exhilarating than to gaze up at the stars, feeling the wind caressing me like a lover through my clothes. I pulled off my hat, unplaited my hair and watched it dance about my face.

"Darling!" said Roger, embracing me. "I hope you weren't frightened."

"Not more than was warranted," I replied. "Thank you."

"James" approached, smiling as though to put the best face on things. "Martin," said Roger, "'tis time for my bride to call you by your true name. Emily, meet Martin Bonnyshanks, First Mate."

"Charmed," I told him.

Martin bowed deeply, then turned his attention to Roger, who wrapped him in his arms. The two men were soon kissing as though they wished to devour each other. Discreetly watching them whilst pretending to study the constellations in the sky, I saw one of Roger's arms reach down until he grasped a plump buttock in one hand. Martin clearly enjoyed the attention, and shifted his weight so that his flesh was pressed into the fingers that would surely leave an imprint on Martin's skin.

I knew then that men could be as sensual as women. I felt both moved and bereft as the reality of my situation was borne in on me. On this ship, I would be as set apart as a mermaid. And unless some man found a way to violate my privacy from malicious curiosity, I would be as chaste as a nun.

Returning to present reality, both my sworn protectors smiled dreamily at me. I couldn't find it in my heart to begrudge them their joy in each other's company.

"Our good ship must be christened," Sir Roger announced to all within earshot, "but we have no champagne, so rum must serve." Even so, the man he ordered to fetch a bottle from the deck-house was clearly offended at the prospect of sacrificing good drink to the sea. "I name thee the *Black Swan*, under God's protection," my husband declared, flourishing the bottle. He smashed it on the rail, and a spray of liquid and glass fell onto the deck and over the hull. A subdued cheer went up.

One man remained at the wheel and others went to their assigned posts, whilst the rest disappeared below decks to indulge their various appetites.

Roger and Martin treated me to a tour of the ship. They proudly explained the firepower of the forty carronades, neglecting to mention that the new ironclads sported more efficient weaponry.

In each section of the ship, I was introduced to the men there. Dujour the Cook was busy in the galley. "Madame la Couturière," he said with energy, "it is an *honneur* to have you wit' us." He glanced downward and added, "Your trousers are *très chic*." He kissed my hand.

"*Je ne suis—*" I began. But what was my role on this ship? I knew that sea travel loses its novelty within days, and that our journey would take weeks if we stayed on course. Otherwise it would take longer, if we reached land again at all. I had brought a writing pad, a pen and a few paints, but I would have a lot of time to fill before (as I secretly hoped) I could prove my worth in hand-to-hand combat.

And the sails needed to be kept in good repair. It seemed I was to be a seamstress after all.

Jackson the Second Mate looked startled when presented with me face-to-face. He remarked drily that leg-o-mutton sleeves no longer seemed as fashionable as they once were, and he guessed that I agreed with him.

Sweeper the Bosun was short, compact and surly. "'Ere, what are you playing at, girl?" he asked me. "Ain't you got your own clothes? What happened to the bloke you stole these from?"

Roger moved to seize Sweeper by the ear, but stopped himself. "This lady is my wife, Sweeper, and my crew will treat her with courtesy on this ship."

"Your crew," sneered the short man. "Your wife. Beg pardon, Sir, but this—woman is your wife by law, no more than that. And then there's Bonnyshanks here. What a Turkish harem you have, Sir."

Sweeper looked up at Roger, who laughed indulgently. Sweeper couldn't prevent his pain from showing in his large gray eyes. I could see that his bad temper was caused by hopeless love for his captain.

I thought of Lucy, and wondered why love must so often be suffered alone. I couldn't help pitying Sweeper, even when he caught my eye and made an unmistakable gesture behind Sir Roger's back. And I couldn't help wondering if he harbored a deeper secret than his *mal de coeur*.

I SPENT THE FIRST NIGHT, AND MOST NIGHTS thereafter, on a pallet in the captain's cabin for safety, while Roger and Martin danced a kind of horizontal jig that made their hammock swing. Although I could not see every detail of their coupling, their grunts and movements gave them away. The two men seemed clumsier and more forceful than women, and I marveled at the things that gave them pleasure.

But then, I thought, they were not blessed with women's soft skin, inviting curves, and hot wet cunnies. As I slid a hand between my thighs, trying to adapt my movements to those of the ship, I wondered how many other women yearned for forbidden pleasure. It was a strangely comforting idea.

Four

Menage a Trois

WHEN WE HAD BEEN A WEEK AT SEA, MARTIN took pity on me and invited me to join them. The touch, the scent and the sight of a vaguely-imagined female lover (part Lucy, part Queen of the Island) still haunted me, but I persuaded myself that sex with Lucy's brother would be an indirect tribute to her. I hoped that she could feel my passion, wherever she was—and with whomever.

"Emily, you will make me a happy man if you give yourself to me," said Roger. "I'm completely sincere. You consented to marry me, after all, and we don't want you to be left alone in the corner. Do we, Martin?"

Martin became exceedingly red, as usual. "If Emily—I mean to say, it is entirely her choice." He looked at me. "Your choice, dear. I am at your service." I guessed that he had never been intimate with a woman before. I would come to learn that both men were more experienced than I had imagined.

My heart filled with affection for both my unlikely suitors. I realized then that love exists in as many different types and degrees as there are colors in the sky and the sea. "You're both generous," I told them, smiling. "And honestly, I'm starved for it."

Roger wrapped me in his arms, and gave me a gentle kiss that carried a hint of fire. I immediately felt like a match that has been struck. "Oh," I gasped, pulling away, "but I really don't want to become a mother. Not yet. I hope you don't—"

"Emily," smiled Roger, "we understand you, and we quite agree. No offense taken. We have too much in hand to invite more difficulty into our lives. Never fear, dear." He winked. "We know how to give you all the pleasure you can bear with no distressing consequences."

"If you wish," muttered Martin. He cleared his throat. "Emily, we shall both close our eyes whilst you undress."

"Don't be silly, Martin," I told him. I couldn't help feeling amused at his discomfort. "If we're going to do this at all, we must do it properly. We must have no secrets from each other." I began to unbutton my shirt, holding his gaze with mine.

Dear Reader, please don't judge me for surrendering what was left of my virtue for the sake of friendship. I did not love my husband or his lover in the way that good women in our time were expected to love men—more than life itself!—but then little about my marriage satisfied the requirements of Society.

I handed my mannish garments to Martin, one at a time, and he occupied himself by folding them carefully. I soon stood barefooted and as naked as Eve on the slippery wooden deck, watching my two suitors studying my form in the flickering light from a lantern. I could feel the vibrations of the ship in my legs and even in my small, sensitive breasts.

I didn't need to ask which man would be my first. "Emily, darling," said Roger, approaching me with arms outspread. He scooped me into his embrace and lifted me off my feet. He raised me until my face was even with his, then he kissed me with all the restrained passion that any female lover of novels might hope for.

Laying me in his hammock, Roger smiled at Martin, who still stood with my clothes in his arms like a laundress. "Come on, man," said my husband. "Don't deprive her of your favors."

As Roger left burning kisses down my throat to my breasts, holding me close, I felt Martin stroking my legs, moving higher up my thighs until his fingers were in the curly hair that barely covered my moistening cleft. Seemingly on impulse, Martin pushed his nose right into my wetness as though my nectar were as necessary to him as milk to a baby. "Don't be afraid, dear," he told me, although he had no reason to think me reluctant.

Roger stroked my hair while nuzzling my breasts. Martin grasped my buttocks in both hands like a jolly sailor with a woman on the town, and lapped at my wet folds with a broad tongue until I squirmed under him in almost unbearable ecstasy. Both men seemed delighted with my responses.

Roger squeezed each of my breasts in turn, and stroked my nipples until I could feel them harden. I struggled to get enough air into my lungs. I could feel my pulse beating time in my puckered nubs, and Roger sucked them into his mouth as though to give them relief.

I was on the point of spending, but I controlled my feelings until I could determine whether Roger, my bridegroom, would really deflower me—assuming that neither Lucy nor I had done this already.

My guess was well-founded. Martin spread my thighs apart, then backed away as Roger placed himself over me, one hand on his red prick to guide it into my waiting cunny. He was as much a gentleman as I could reasonably expect, but before I could fully accept his large sword in my scabbard, I felt such a burning pain inside that I instinctively jerked upward, further impaling myself. "Oh!" I heard myself shout.

"Shh!" replied both men at once. They were clearly more conscious of an unseen audience of listening ears than I was.

"Easy, dear," Roger told me. His voice in my ear sounded sympathetic, but with a note of masculine pride as well. "I'm all the way in. I won't be long."

I thought him altogether too long and too thick, but soon the pain inside me mellowed into a heat that heightened my excitement.

"Ahh," breathed Roger, jerking his prick out of me with rude haste. A fountain of white spunk erupted from the tiny slit in the prick's head like champagne bursting from its bottle, and baptized my belly. "Thank God," he swore. "That was close. I'm sorry, Emily, but you cast a spell on me. I could hardly control myself."

Roger's prick softened to a less intimidating size, but it still bore streaks of red. I knew that my maidenhead must be well and truly gone.

Had I ever really hoped to live the life of a respectable woman? At that point, I couldn't be sure. I reminded myself that no one could ever blame me for submitting to my bridegroom on our honeymoon. No one.

But was I truly married? And if so, could I ever be the true lover of a woman—Lucy, of course, if she'd have me—if I returned to England alive? It was too much to contemplate.

I no longer felt Martin touching me anywhere, but his disappointment was palpable. Looking over Roger's shoulder, I saw Martin standing upright against the wall, wearing a forlorn expression.

"Help me, Martin." I begged, wanting to give him as much comfort as I hoped he would give me. "I need your tongue."

Roger moved aside, allowing Martin to take his place. Martin showed his skill at soothing my tender slit with his tongue, and he seemed sincerely interested in my female parts. I surmised that he had sailed in such waters before.

"Emily, you needn't let me board you again," Roger assured me, stroking my hair as though to pull my attention upward from where Martin was licking me so deliciously.

Martin raised his head and gave Roger a meaningful look. "Board me, guv'nor," he said.

Roger laughed. "I will, me hearty," he responded, "but the law must be satisfied." I understood. My marriage to Roger could not have been legal had it not been consummated.

I wondered if Martin could be satisfied by bathing my nether parts with his tongue. I became aware of my own selfishness when I felt the touch of his stiff rod, demanding attention. I tried to fit my hand around it, but in my present position, that proved an impossible feat. "You may pet my stallion later, dear," he told me.

"Allow me," offered Roger in a voice that rippled with barely-suppressed humor. He seized one of my hips and pulled me onto my side, briefly displacing Martin, who quickly relocated my little button of flesh with his fingers, and fastened his mouth upon it. As Martin gently teased me with his teeth and lashed me with his strong, pointed tongue, I felt Roger's warm hand sliding down my backside. Without warning, he smacked one of my lower cheeks so smartly that the sound echoed against the walls of our small chamber.

"Ohh!" I squealed, this time in pleasure and surprise. Martin clung to me as I spent in his mouth.

"Good wench!" laughed my husband. "Life in the Navy suits her," he told Martin.

But Martin had not reached his own climax. If our odd ménage was going to work at all, it had to be fair.

Trying to change my position in the hammock was a disastrous experiment that almost pitched me face-down onto the deck. My scramble to capture Martin's fine, thick rod was ultimately successful, however. "Uh," he groaned, lying on his back with his manhood sticking proudly up at me. I circled it with my fingers, and stroked it until it grew as hard as a steel rod in a silk sheath.

Remembering how well Martin had driven me to distraction, I took his rod into my mouth and licked the head. I grazed it with my teeth as lightly as I could, but the combined movements of the ship and the man under me forced his rod so deeply into my throat that I choked, gasped and pulled away.

"Allow me," repeated Roger in the tone of an indulgent teacher. He bent over Martin, lowered his mouth onto Martin's prick, and sucked until his cheeks hollowed.

"Ah, man!" groaned Martin, and soon I could tell that his crisis had come. Roger sucked and swallowed until Martin's prick was as deflated as a sail without wind.

"I'll do it next time, Martin," I promised. "I want to." At the moment, however, I had no desire to try it again.

All three of us tried to fit our bodies together in the hammock like puppies in a basket. Our efforts were doomed. No matter which man tried to hold me close to his chest while pressed against his lover, someone was always in danger of being pitched out of bed.

I imagined two women wrapped neatly in each other's arms without a glimmer of light between their two bodies, snug in a hammock. In that case, I thought, the fit would be perfect.

At length, I offered a solution. "Good night, husbands," I whispered, trying to leave the hammock without disturbing its other occupants. "I'll be nearby."

"Good night, dear wife," said Roger.

"Good night, Emily dear," said Martin. I crawled to my pallet, and curled up on it. I thought I heard a mutual sigh of relief from both men.

THE FOLLOWING NIGHT, I MANFULLY (SO to speak) took Martin's cock into my mouth as he lay in the hammock alone while Roger paced the deck, charting the ship's progress. I used my hands to caress Martin's hairy balls and the base of his cock while licking the head with my tongue. "Emily!" he exclaimed, showing his appreciation in the most obvious ways. I enjoyed the sense of utter control that the act gave me, but Martin was soon thrusting hard in my mouth, despite his efforts to slow down.

He groaned aloud as a stream of his jism filled my mouth, and I could not see a polite alternative to swallowing it. How different it was from a woman's love-juice! As soon as I released him, Martin pulled me into his arms and kissed me. He seemed overwhelmed with relief and gratitude. I was glad to get such a reception, but I hoped he wouldn't expect such service every night of our voyage.

I fell asleep on my pallet before Roger returned to the cabin that night, and awoke in the dark to the sounds of my two husbands making a ruckus in their hammock.

Several nights later, curiosity and my sense of fairness prompted me to unbutton Roger's trousers to find the sausage I hadn't tasted yet. "I want to see it, Roger," I told him.

"Then you shall, my dear," he told me. He removed his clothing faster than I could do it, and showed me his rod, which hardened even before I touched it. I knelt before it, finding that position easier to maintain than a cramped spot in the hammock. Roger held his rod still until I covered it with my mouth, but it was so large that I could only take in half its length. My tongue soon encouraged it to grow even larger in sudden jerks. It felt as hard as the mast of our ship.

"You're a lucky girl, Emily," said Martin, standing behind me and holding me in place.

Roger groaned in pleasure, and jerked once, twice, thrice. His essence filled my mouth, and it tasted as salty as the ocean surrounding us. I couldn't bring myself to swallow it. I let my husband's seed spill down my chin and onto my shirt, my trousers, his boots and the deck.

"Tsk," commented Martin. "What a shambles."

Roger gently eased his manhood out of my mouth and gave it a few strokes as it spewed its last load. He produced a handkerchief from somewhere, and solicitously wiped my face with it before using it to dry his rod as much as possible. "Emily dear," he laughed. "You constantly amaze us. She's quite a cocksucker, isn't she, Martin?"

"Oh, quite." He couldn't keep the sarcasm out of his voice as he pulled me up by my armpits.

"I want us all to be the best of friends," I explained. I was afraid I sounded idiotic, but I didn't know how better to express my intentions. A comic image of Roger, Martin and me as the Three Musketeers sprang into my mind.

Roger wrapt his arms about me and pulled me close. "You'll always be safe with us, dear heart," he promised.

"Thank you, Roger," I said, adding pointedly: "and Martin." I sighed, and tried to exit the hammock gracefully. I told my suitors: "Now you must excuse me because I'm just dropping off." Each of them kissed me good night. I felt their relief and impatience, even whilst I felt their love like sunlight on my skin. I knew they both craved each other's touch, and as much privacy as I could give them.

I fell asleep on my pallet, but I was wakened in the early hours by the sounds of a hushed conversation.

"Rodge," said Martin, his voice muffled by Roger's body, "if...if we ever return to England..." I heard him take a ragged breath. "When you and your jolly wife return to your family seat...what shall I be to you? Will you hire me to keep the grounds? Tutor your children?"

I heard the baritone of Roger's voice, pitched too low to be heard by anyone but the man he held next to his heart. Listening carefully, I heard "love," "you," and "patience, man." I cursed the cruelty of the conventions that would force my two husbands to hide their mutual passion for the rest of their lives—if they could bear to do it. And I would not be here, I reminded myself, if those same conventions had not forced my Lucy into a loveless arrangement with a man of her parents' choice.

"Martin," I whispered. Two pairs of eyes turned toward me in the darkness. "Don't trouble yourself on my account. We three have an understanding. Don't we?"

"We do, Emily." I only heard Roger's voice, but I sensed Martin's hope that he could rely on my sympathy. From then on, I kept to my pallet at night except when one of the men invited me to join them. I usually awoke more rested than they were.

BY DAYLIGHT, I AFFORDED BOTH MEN SOME amusement when I tried on their clothes to discover which I could wear. Martin's were too large altogether, while Roger's were too long in the trouser-legs and the sleeves, but he gave me a set of clothes to be altered to fit me. I felt as well-dressed as anyone else on board.

During the first fortnight of our journey, the sea was a glassy plain, disturbed only by gliding shapes below and flocks of quarrelling sea-birds who dove down from above. Each night as darkness fell, men gathered to play their pipes and whistles and to dance the jigs and reels of their own home-towns. There was liquor enough to light fires in their eyes as well as in their loins.

The Green Men were like the "army of lovers" of ancient poetry. Our little republic functioned well enough, although flogging was more often meted out as a reward than as discipline. The promise of stimulation in a stirring scene seemed to ensure general diligence and co-operation just as well as the threat of pain.

The morality of the Green Men's Society was largely a mystery to me, and I sometimes considered it, alone on my pallet, in the moments before sleep overcame me. Was anything truly evil to them? (The image of a hangman's noose came to my mind.) What would most of them experience as true punishment? (I imagined a monk's solitary cell.)

I resolved to learn as much about my sailing companions as I could through observation.

Shelter from the Storm

DESPITE THE BEAUTY OF SUNLIGHT ON WATER
and the bracing salt wind, sea travel was as uncomfortable as
I remembered from my childhood. Fresh water was in short
supply, and everything on board was wet, sticky or oily to
the touch. Three days after our departure, I used my sewing
scissors to cut my hair as short as a man's.

At night, bedbugs shared my pallet, and rats could be
heard scuttling out of sight. And for five days in a month, I
had rags to clean. Freedom always comes at a cost.

AS I STOOD AT THE RAILS, ADMIRING THE VIEW,
or wandered about the ship in search of occupation, men
consulted me about fashion and adornment. Could I make
a gentleman's waistcoat out of brocade, assuming there was
some to be had in the Bahamas? Would I consider making a lady's gown to a man's dimensions out of an old sail
which could be dyed a beautiful dark blue once indigo was
procured? Did I think pearl or diamond jewelry to be better
suited to a rather sallow complexion? Did I not think that
parting one's hair exactly in the middle made one's nose look
too long?

Watching the clouds, my companions sighed about the vir-
tues of fine cotton: its softness against the skin, its delightful

smell when freshly-ironed, its fluidity, its elegance, and its scarcity since the beginning of the American war.

EARLY IN OUR VOYAGE, I ASKED ROGER AND Martin about our mission. "Husbands," I asked them, "are we to settle in the Bahamas? And how shall we survive?"

Martin cleared his throat. "We may do, Emily," he told me, "but first we need to intercept a blockade-runner."

Roger had explained to me that the attempts of the Union government to cut off supplies to the Confederacy were regularly thwarted by cleverly-manned schooners from the southern states which sailed to Nassau to trade cotton and tobacco for items more useful to the southerners. He hadn't told me that few of the Green Men valued the life of a freed slave more than a bale of cotton or a pound of tobacco.

"Cotton?" I shrieked, completely out of sorts. "Are we sailing to the New World just to steal a shipload of bloody cotton? Are you raving mad?"

"Get hold of yourself, Emily," admonished Roger. "Have you never heard of expeditions to the Far East for spices and silk? Some adventurers made fortunes for themselves and improved the lives of all their countrymen. And cotton is not all we need. Tobacco, especially in a good cigar, makes men more amiable. The best physicians attest to this. Green Men aren't Spartans, dear. We need beauty and pleasure as much as we need air."

His argument was persuasive, if lacking in moral rigor. So we were not all set on defending universal freedom after all.

Now I knew that I could earn my own fortune as a dressmaker for men, who would pay me in coin and in adoration if I could dress them in ladies' attire—and gentlemen's suits as well. For an instant, I imagined myself as a designer to rival Monsieur Worth in Paris. I could ease my conscience by repaying my parents for the extraordinary expense of my education, which had caused them hardship.

Before then, however, the Green Men and I needed to become warriors. I had seen the swords and shorter knives that my two men kept in their cabin.

"I want you both to practice sword-fighting with me," I told them. "We must all be prepared if we mean to take over a Confederate ship. We can't rely solely on our smashers. We don't know what weapons the Americans carry—and we need to beware of both sides."

And so, on balmy afternoons, I squinted against the flash of sun on steel as the clang of swords echoed against the wooden fittings of the ship. Sometimes I dueled with Roger, and sometimes with Martin, who was graceful and light-footed for his size. As I felt myself gaining strength, speed and cunning, I thought of Lucy and determined to gain such a heroic reputation that no one in England could keep her away from me.

Meanwhile, Sweeper watched me from the corners.

ONE MORNING AS I EMERGED FROM THE captain's cabin, he seized me from behind, pressing a broom-handle against my throat until I began to swoon. Desperately, I pried his fingers off the wood, twisted quickly and thrust my knee into his crotch with all the force I could muster.

My blow reached its target, but Sweeper didn't recoil in pain. "He don't love you, wench!" babbled the man, reaching out to throttle me. I stomped on one of his feet, lowered one shoulder and threw myself at his chest. "Oofff," grunted Sweeper, staggering against the deck-house.

For a moment, neither of us had enough breath to speak. And then we spoke at once. "You damn fool!" shouted Sweeper.

"You idiot!" I shouted back. "Of course he doesn't love me! I don't love him either! Not as a wife, if that's what you mean. And I know you're a woman. I've known all this time!"

The rage leaked out of my opponent like air from a pricked balloon. "You don't love him!" he (or she) repeated in wonder. "Why joo marry him then?"

"For appearances," I explained. "I love someone else, if you must know."

Sweeper was still trying to fill his/her lungs, but s/he grinned slyly. "Oho, I can guess who. I heard your confabs with Jackson."

"You're completely mistaken," I explained, as if to a child. "You don't know how much I miss the one I dream of. She's a woman."

Sweeper looked quizzical. "A lady-love," she said with amazement. "Missus Emily—I never guessed."

I became aware that we were still holding onto each other, trying to prevent another outbreak of hostilities. Sweeper and I were approximately the same size, but her arms felt as strong as a man's. I wondered what those arms would feel like if she ever held me with affection.

"Sweeper!" jeered one of the men. "Where d'you hide yer bubbies?"

"Show us your quim!" shouted someone else. We were surrounded by an audience that had been attracted by the commotion.

"I'll show you how real men fuck!" offered another man.

I felt as if a powder-keg had just rolled onto the deck. I was sure I was not the first on board to have guessed Sweeper's secret (either or both of them), but now that her gender was no longer a mystery, those who might have danced a hornpipe with her in private stood to be exposed as secret cuntlovers, or traitors to their kind.

"Fuck you all!" she shouted. "I hope you all hang! You can go to hell!"

Faster than it takes to tell, Sweeper pulled a hunting-knife from somewhere in her trousers, and stuck it in the belly of the man who had told her to show her quim. Blood gushed from the wound and dripped on the deck as he staggered backward, too shocked to utter a sound.

Roger and Martin appeared, pistols drawn. "Bones," ordered Roger, "attend to this man here." The Medical Purser helped the wounded man (whose name was Hopwell) to the sick bay below deck.

For a moment I wondered if our crew, all suffering from cabin fever and a frustrated desire for action, would erupt in mutiny. Luckily, the presence of Roger and Martin seemed to bring them back to their senses. Every man was ordered back to his duties except Sweeper, whose mates were ordered to take over the cleaning of the ship—which, as Roger pointed out, had not been done thoroughly since we left port. Sweeper was taken to the brig by two men who undoubtedly gave her a few thumps to remember them by.

We had a wounded man on board and we were running low on supplies. We needed to make port soon, or find a ship carrying booty, preferably one with no guns at all.

THE NEXT NIGHT, I PERSUADED ROGER AND Martin to let me bring Sweeper to our cabin and confine her there. The quarters were cramped enough already and my two husbands had no desire to share them with two women, but they saw the logic of my plea: that leaving her anywhere else would invite the men's revenge, and lead to anarchy.

And so I found myself sharing a pallet with another female, to define her in the most physical sense. For the first few days, Sweeper's bitterness seemed to fill our cabin as she sat or paced silently, staring hot-eyed into space.

As I continued to write my story about the Queen of the Island, Sweeper whittled a piece of wood into the shape of a crude whistle, then blew into it until she made a sound like the call of a distressed bird, perhaps a wounded albatross.

"Clever," I told her, trying not to laugh. "Can you play a tune?"

"Wot it's for," she replied. She blew into her little instrument, then carefully carved more space for air to flow through it. At length she was able to play a tune that sounded like "Danny Boy," and the notes resounded against the walls of our little chamber. The song had its own simple charm.

"Sweeper," I asked, "did you always know you wanted to be a man? Or a boy when you were young?"

"Aye." She was willing to tell me her tale, but not to look me in the eyes. "All me brothers were allowed to stay out of doors until all hours whilst me mum taught me to sew and bake. Didn't seem fair."

"I agree, but being kept indoors isn't really about having female parts. Bosun's work on a ship isn't very different from housekeeping, you know. We'll all have to fight when the time comes."

"P'raps it's different for you, Miss Emily." She gazed at me with sea-gray eyes that showed a certain masculine boldness and honesty. "I wanted to join the Navy and be just like the other blokes."

Her breasts must have been tightly bound beneath her shirt, because no feminine swelling could be seen. I wondered if the binding affected her breathing. She had done a remarkable job of presenting herself as the person she wanted to be, and I couldn't help admiring her efforts.

I also couldn't help wanting to see her without a stitch of clothing. I asked her, "Did you ever give yourself a proper name besides 'Sweeper'?"

"Alfred," she told me. "A good old name, 'tis. Wish me parents had christened me that."

"It sounds kingly," I assured her. "I'll call you Alfred when we're alone." I thought of something else. "If you always wanted to be just like other blokes, did you ever go ashore with your mates to find a wench?"

In reply, Sweeper played a tune with a merry rhythm and several discordant notes.

"I know who you fancy. It's not a secret, lad," I told her. "I'm just wondering if you could fancy a woman. On the side, as it were."

She set her whistle aside and gave me a devilish grin. "I have something you'd like," she told me. "I made it meself, and it would pass inspection in the dark."

"I'd like to try it, Sweeper, really I would. Wait until night, and our cabin-mates will be too distracted to notice. I could please you too, and it wouldn't make you less of who you are. Whilst we're sharing quarters, we can share a few harmless pleasures."

I offered her both my hands, and she rose to her feet just as the ship rolled unexpectedly, and threw me against her chest. She kissed me, and I responded with a sigh. It had been too long since anyone with a completely hairless face had kissed me with interest.

I could still summon Lucy's sparkling eyes and glossy dark ringlets to the private cabin of my imagination, but the knife-edge of my longing had been blunted since my last sight of her. I couldn't forget how easily she had acceded to her parents' wishes, not only to accept a suitor but to banish me from her life. In fairness, I thought (searching my memory for every scrap of evidence in the case), I had ended our relationship myself. I honestly didn't know whether I could apologize to her and try to begin again, even if she were still unattached.

School had been a place apart, and we could never go back there to live.

Alfred and I couldn't wait for nightfall to consummate our growing friendship. We lowered ourselves to our pallet, where I held her against my breasts. "Ah, girl," she moaned. "You're a fine one." I felt hot tears wetting my neck, and knew they came from her.

"I need to feel your skin, lover," I told her. "'Twon't work any other way." As shyly as a maiden on her wedding-night, she rose up enough to pull off her shirt and unwrap her bindings. Her breasts were scarcely bigger than well-developed muscles in a man's bosom, but they marked her as a member of my own sex.

I removed my own shirt so that we would be equally exposed. I knew we were missing the evening meal, but I needed the nourishment she could give me. She helped me to slide my manly trousers down my womanly haunches, and then I returned the favor. She smiled at the damp triangle of matted curls between my thighs as she proudly thrust out her own crotch. There a kind of leather sausage stuck out from a harness about her hips.

Her device looked like a parody of what every man takes for granted. I knew that most of the Green Men (even my husbands?) would laugh scornfully, but I didn't care. I was moved by Sweeper's resourcefulness and determination to furnish for herself what nature had neglected to provide.

We lay together, and the smooth weight of her makeshift cock pressed against my thighs. I kissed her mouth, her cheeks and her dewy neck, breathing in her earthy scent. She held my breasts and teased my nipples until they felt as hard as bullets. "Show me your behind, lass," she commanded. "'Tis the most natural position."

I positioned myself on hands and knees on the slippery floor of the cabin, hoping I could hold steady for as long as possible. I felt her small, rough fingers stroking my arsecheeks. Nothing could have given me more pleasure at that moment, except what followed. Two of her fingers slid down the crack of my derrière until they found the hair round my quim. Without hesitation, they plunged into it.

"Ohh—" I moaned in ecstasy, resisting the impulse to shout. "Alfred! That feels so good."

Chuckling, she explored my wet folds and stroked my little button. I almost squirmed out of her grasp, and she used two fingers to hold and pinch it as it swelled. "Don't spend yet, sweetheart," she warned me.

Her thighs pressed against mine as she pushed her leather cock into me. I pushed back to get as much of it as I could, and my hips rocked of their own accord.

She grasped me with strong, slim fingers that seemed likely to leave marks on my skin when we were finished. She thrust once, twice, thrice, to find a depth and a rhythm which would please us both, and she settled into a delicious pattern of in-and-out.

When she squeezed my little button again, I erupted like a fountain, clutching her makeshift cock over and over as a stream of my essence wet the wooden planks under me. "Ahhh!" I groaned as quietly as I could. I could feel Sweeper's satisfaction as she wrapped her arms round my hips and belly.

"Alfred," I murmured. "You're man enough for me." She ran a warm hand along my back, then planted little nibbly kisses on my backside.

After she withdrew her love-tool, Sweeper helped me to crawl to my pallet, where we lay pressed as tightly together as we could. We were both bathed in sweat as we breathed in the natural aromas of each other's bodies. I felt as tranquil in Sweeper's arms as a swallow in her own nest.

We kissed languidly, enjoying the experience. I rubbed her shoulders and felt her relax almost imperceptibly. "You're the girl for me, Emily," she told me gravely, speaking into my ear. She seemed happier than I had ever seen her, although I knew she was still under my husband's spell. The voice and presence of the Captain would never lose their power over her.

By subtle degrees, I turned her in my arms and kissed my way down her sturdy back. When I reached her buttocks, I kneaded them like a cat. "Let me please you, Alfred," I begged. "No one else shall ever know." She didn't answer in words, but she moved her hips in an unmistakable way. My daring fingers found their way under her harness and touched the warm dew of her very private garden. With a sigh, she allowed me to stroke her secret flesh and the little man that mimicked the one she had made for herself.

I felt her quaking response to my attention, and her intense relief when the cataclysm struck. Oh, Sweeper! How could I ever persuade you that womanhood is an excellent state for those who can see it? But for your sake, I wish you could have had the manhood you wanted.

For many nights thereafter, "Alfred" and I took comfort from each other, and she seemed grateful for my company. After all, I was the wife of the one she wanted and could never have, just as Roger shared a dear blood-tie with my lost Lucy.

I was privileged to touch every inch of her body, but this was a ritual not to be spoken of or acknowledged in words. Like the man she wounded, I was never privileged to see her quim in the light, or even her tightly-bound "bubbies." I valued the limited trust she gave to me.

I understood that Sweeper and I, our husbands and the rest of the Green Men were all on a journey which was not simply a mad quest for pleasure. Love comes in many forms, and it is no less real when it is less than perfect.

Engagement

FOR WEEKS, MY DREAMS WERE TROUBLED by images of a woman who seemed to embody the spirit of our figurehead, the black swan. Whilst dreaming, I heard a musical voice calling to me like that of a mermaid from the deeps: "Emily! Come find me!" In some dreams, a dark woman showed herself to me in a flowing scarlet gown which dissolved into a fluid which looked like blood, which in turn dissolved into the water in which she swam, leaving her naked. She was tall and slim, and her skin shone bronze, copper or gold when touched by sunlight in its various moods.

I knew that the world of dry land was full of women: old and young, pink, tan, golden, brown and Nubian black. I could still easily remember my classmates, English rosebuds all, in a school where men and lads seemed as strange and faintly sinister as fauns or gargoyles. I could remember my mother's parlor filled with the skirts and bonnets of female visitors.

And now I was confined to a ship where I was the only specimen of my sex who did not yearn to be something else. Some days, I felt like the last of my tribe, or the last dinosaur on earth.

One evening, as I lingered on deck with my mending in hand, I heard one of the Green Men singing to a circle of his mates:

O the dark maid in the midnight glade
Where the moon doth never shine,
She lies in wait both soon and late
Drinking the reddest wine.

All men beware to find her there,
On the banks of a deep, deep lake,
Who seeks her out will ne'er come out,
And their loved ones' hearts will break.

This old song, sung to frighten children into staying close by the family hearth, now simply put me out of sorts. Perhaps, thought I, if any of the woods or lakes of Great Britain (which presently seemed infinitely safer than the trackless ocean) were inhabited by a "dark maid," she might have more reason to be afraid of the men who sought her out than they of her. I let my fancy conjure up the image of a young woman with skin like gleaming ebony, running from a pack of men like a desperate fox seeking sanctuary from the hunt.

Such a woman would feel more closely related to wild things than to her pursuers. She would learn the secrets of wild places and establish cordial relations with foxes, badgers, moles, otters, even birds and snakes. She would learn which plants are poisonous and which are medicinal.

Such a woman would pray to all the old gods of fen and mountain, lake and stream. She would become dangerous to those who would seek to harm her. She would shun all company but another woman who would patiently, fearlessly, wait for her to show herself.

I wanted to offer my love to an unconquered woman who would find me worthy. For now, I could only dream.

ON A DAY OF OPPRESSIVE HEAT, THE MONO-tony of my life was finally broken. "Land!" shouted a man in the crow's-nest. We all gathered on deck to see a speck of green on the horizon, and Jackson was pleased to tell us that it was the island of New Providence, a center for contraband trade.

Before we could reach the island, a schooner came into view, making fast progress over the waves. Her sails billowed in the wind like petticoats on a clothesline. Enlarged in a spyglass, her name appeared as the *Dixieland*.

For a moment, I wished to make the acquaintance of another shipload of men, new and possibly interesting personalities. I reminded myself, however, that we had not crossed the wide ocean to attend an "at-home."

To my amazement, a party of our crew hoisted a Union Jack up the mainmast. Someone had had the foresight to stow it away for this occasion.

We were soon close enough to parley with the officers of the smaller ship. "Ho there!" shouted a fellow in a brass-buttoned jacket, waving with lanky hands that protruded considerably from the sleeves. "State your name and your business!"

"Captain James Featherlight of the *Black Swan*," boasted Martin. Roger remained below deck. "Her Majesty, Queen Victoria of Great Britain and the Empire, offers friendship to the Confederate States of America."

There seemed to be a hurried conference on the other ship. "Captain Gregory Towne," shouted the man in the ill-fitting jacket. "Welcome! Do you bring supplies?"

"We bring arms," answered Martin. Our gunports were revealed so that our smashers could be seen in all their glory. "Have you cotton or tobacco?"

"Do you wish to trade?" asked Captain Towne.

"Aye!" Martin responded. In his excitement, he looked as red as a boiled lobster. "Give us your goods, and you may escape with your lives."

As I feared, the schooner was also armed, but we had superior size and firepower. "Never!" shouted the other captain, waving furiously as though to push us back out to sea. He consulted with his fellow-officers as our men scrambled into position.

"Fire!" we heard from the other ship just as Roger gave the same order on ours.

A ball came whistling through the air to tear a hole in one of our sails, leaving it flapping raggedly in the breeze. At the same time, one of our balls blasted through the bow of the schooner.

I wondered how many men on the Confederate ship had their own version of the Green Men's Society. I wondered if their newly-formed government had strict laws against male cohabitation, as did ours.

The savagery of the law made no sense to me. Neither did the propensity of men of all nations and religions to seize any excuse to attack those who are really not much different from themselves.

As amazing as it was to me that our men were prepared to kill the southerners for their cotton, I was dumbfounded that they were prepared to die in its defense. I failed to see any nobility in this version of "honor."

Yet a good fight was much more exciting than the routine of life at sea. For a moment, I amused myself by trying to translate "Better to die in war than die of boredom" into a stirring Latin slogan that schoolchildren could be forced to memorize.

The next ball from the schooner missed one of our masts by inches. Our next ball further damaged their hull, leaving a splintered hole in the wood. The ship was taking on water.

A man on the schooner's deck frantically waved a white flag. "Clemency, sirs!" he begged. "We accept your terms!"

I feared a trap, but most of the Green Men were deaf to reason. With a series of loud cheers, they threw grappling hooks onto the schooner as merrily as wedding guests throwing rice. When the two ships were securely joined, a row of Green Men rushed onto the *Dixieland*, whooping and laughing.

Martin was more cautious. "Sir!" he shouted. "Assemble your crew on deck."

An assortment of fierce faces, threadbare shirts, jackets, caps and trousers met our sight. More to the point, a row of muskets pointed straight at us. A few of the *Dixieland's* officers held rifles.

A volley of shots rang out, and the results were horrible to watch. One of Sweeper's (as they called her) mates was knocked into the water, and he seemed too wounded to swim. Two of the men who assisted Dujour in the galley screamed and fell to the deck of the schooner. Three men who were still standing quickly tried to return to the *Black Swan*. Another of Sweeper's mates punched one of the American rebels in the face and pulled a knife from his pocket. As a man from the *Dixieland* fired a musket, the knife-wielder plunged his weapon into the shooter's ribs.

"Parley!" shouted Martin. He was ignored by the men on both sides. If indeed the schooner carried cotton and tobacco, this treasure seemed likely to end up at the bottom of the Caribbean Sea with the Green Men of our side who coveted it.

Panic seemed to sharpen my vision. I saw three men on the opposite side of the schooner lowering a skiff into the water, bent on escape. At first, this sight seemed illogical. I scanned the horizon, not really knowing what I sought, and saw a modern ship without sails, approaching under its own power. It flew the flag of the United States of America, called the Yankee flag by southern patriots.

The men on our ship seemed oblivious to anything but their desire to avenge their fallen mates and lovers. "Fire!" shouted Roger. One of our smashers sent a ball into the line of armed men on the *Dixieland*. None were left standing. The deck of the schooner ran red with blood.

Did I swoon at the sight? I did not. The carnage was worse than anything I had seen before in my life, but I had no time to let it distress me. The sun blazed on the scene without mercy, dispersing shadows, and I was grateful that our men could see the enemy clearly. The battle was exhilarating, and I knew that every movement that any of us made could tip the outcome toward victory or defeat.

Roger stood with Sweeper (my Alfred) by his side. They both handed knives to half a dozen men. I had held a sword behind my back since we approached the schooner, but I hoped that I wouldn't need to use it.

Captain Towne lay in a tangle of limbs and exposed flesh, including soft gray inwards and the sharp tips of broken bones. Even if he were still clinging to life, I didn't think he could survive long. The men of his crew who remained unharmed seemed confused and disorganized. One picked up the white flag and waved it until one of his fellows tore it from his hands.

"Peace!" shouted the man who wished to surrender.

"Death before dishonor!" shouted the other.

"Martin, dear," said Roger. "We need to settle the dispute." In a louder voice, he shouted, "Time to board!"

We went over the side by twos and threes, weapons drawn. Sweeper was in the first group, and she climbed the schooner's mast to the yard, which she straddled as confidently as a monkey seated in a palm tree.

The man who valued honor above life held a rifle aimed at Roger's heart. With one graceful movement, Alfred sent her knife hurtling into the would-be shooter's chest.

"'Tis a female!" bellowed a stout man in a torn shirt. I assumed he was referring to Alfred until he was almost upon me, raising his meaty fist. Such was the chivalry of the planters' aristocracy. But then, I hardly appeared to be a gracious lady. I belonged to a pack of thieves who were bent on stealing the ship's cargo.

On that subject, what greater theft could there be than the traffic in human beings, on which the Confederates depended? Perhaps justice was too pure a concept to be found embodied in the real world. And I had no time to cudgel my wits about it.

I kept my uncouth attacker at a distance with my sword. He pulled a knife from beneath one arm, and tried to use it to knock my sword out of my hands. I sent the knife flying across the deck.

The man charged me, both hands raised. I swung my sword, and one hand, still clenched, fell from his wrist in a shower of blood.

Roger and Martin rounded up the remaining men while most of our crew ran below to plunder the cargo. Within minutes, their whoops announced that they had found precious bales of cotton, and tobacco-leaves as fragrant as a sachet of dried flowers amongst the delicate garments in a chest of drawers.

UNTIL THE WHOLE SHIP WAS SEARCHED, WE couldn't be sure exactly what it carried. Holding my sword, I tried to enter a closed cabin, but the door held firm. Throwing myself against it, I splintered the wood without creating an opening. Looking about me, I saw a metal object resembling a boot-scraper, and pounded it against the door until it gave.

A pair of large, dark eyes stared at me in fright. "Dis niggah nevah done nuttin," squeaked a slim mulatto woman whose gown was so covered in blood that the color of the fabric was hard to discern. The wet cotton clung so closely to her body that it was possible to see the exact shape of her high breasts and the nipples that crowned them. On the deck behind her lay a man with a gaping slash in his throat, staring wide-eyed at eternity. "Somebody kilt Masta Fugga. I nevah done nuttin'!"

Her desperate appearance suggested a lifetime of ignorance and mistreatment, but something in her attitude reminded me of Lucy. I sensed that the young woman was playing a role to save her life.

"You're safe now, miss," I promised her. "No one will harm you. You're under the protection of Her Majesty's Navy. Are you injured?"

She shook her head vigorously, as though afraid to speak. "What is your name?" I asked.

She looked behind me, and seemed to realize that I was neither a man myself, nor accompanied by any. She looked me in the eyes without fear or apology, and a growing smile tugged at her full lips. "They call me Mary Ann Cornford," she told me. "My master gave me that name."

I was vaguely aware of the sound of boots running all over a creaky wooden deck, yet an unnerving silence seemed to surround the dark nymph who looked as graceful yet solid as a statue.

Reddest Wine

MARY ANN, AS WE ALL CAME TO KNOW HER, thus showed the presence of mind that never deserted her.

"What shall I call you?" I asked her, wanting to comfort this woman who seemed to have been driven to kill. She showed remarkable *sang-froid*. In fact, she was covered in cooling blood.

"Call me Mary Ann," she replied in a voice like treacle. "My other name tangles up white folks' tongues."

She spoke like the chatelaine of a manor-house in the feudal American South, a land removed from the fast pace of modern civilization.

"Mary Ann," I repeated, reaching for her nearest hand. "I'm Emily. Some day, I hope you will teach me to call you by your true name. You can't stay here. I can lend you cleaner clothes on our ship, the *Black Swan*."

She resisted my grasp. "Do you aim to take me prisoner?" she demanded. "Gal, it'll take more than you to keep me tied up until your captain decides what to do with me."

I wanted to assure her that she was in no danger, but I really didn't know what Roger would do once he became aware of her apparent guilt. The evidence looked damning.

As though summoned by my thoughts, Roger's boots and voice announced his approach. He wrapt an arm protectively about my waist. "Martin," he called over his shoulder, "take them quickly. We want no one left alive on this ship to tell tales." His eyes, as wild as those of an embattled stallion, took in me, Mary Ann and her former companion in a glance. "Good Lord!" he exclaimed.

"This man will tell no tales, sir," said Mary Ann.

"Whatever he was to you, miss, you must come with us now," Roger told her.

"Rodge—Captain sir," called Martin from the deck. "Come here at once! A vessel from the other side."

For an instant, I remembered ghost ships I had heard of, doomed to circle the globe forever to do penance for the actions of their crew. We were surely not the only pirates on the seven seas. Then I remembered that the Yankee steamship must have caught up to us.

"Ahoy!" called a masculine voice. "State your business in these waters."

"Emily, don't let her get away," Roger muttered to me. For several reasons, I didn't want to let Mary Ann out of my sight. Roger dashed out of the cabin.

Restless boots paced the deck. "The *Black Swan* of Her Majesty's Navy offers friendship to the United States of America," called Roger. "We have intercepted a blockade-runner bearing contraband."

A great cheer went up from the nearby ship, punctuated by whistles and the sounds of men clapping their hands and stamping their boots on wet wood. "Well done, England!" called a voice.

"Good for you, boys!" called another.

A shouted exchange of names quickly followed. "Captain John Greenleaf," Roger introduced himself.

"Captain Joshua Swift of the *Martha Washington*," replied his counterpart. "Do you have wounded men on board?"

BEFORE LONG, I HEARD THE INTRUSION OF a great many more feet on our deck as the northerners came aboard to claim the surviving southerners as prisoners of war.

What would happen when the Yankees found Mary Ann? The sight of a dark woman with blood on her hands (and most of the rest of her) would not appeal to their sense of chivalry, assuming they had it.

My conscience was troubled. I knew from experience that a white child can appear more innocent than she is, but the sentimental notions that saved me in my youth could not be passed to a dark woman like a protective cloak.

As I watched in shock, Mary Ann pulled her blood-soaked gown above her head and threw it aside. For a moment, she stood clad in a chemise that clung to her. She quickly removed it, and used the few dry spots on her clothing to wipe the blood from her *café-au-lait* skin, now completely exposed from her enigmatic face to her elegant collarbone to her breasts to her belly to the triangle of curly black hair that stopped my gaze. I was entranced.

The naked beauty studied the dead man at her feet as though to determine whether any of his clothing could be salvaged, but it was as blood-soaked as her own. Her expressive eyes roamed about the small cabin and landed on a filthy neckerchief which was almost the same color as the planks it lay upon. She snatched it up and held it below her navel, her arms crossed over her breasts. Her attempts to cover herself were in vain.

A blue-uniformed man entered the cabin and stopped as though turned to stone.

"Please, sir!" squealed Mary Ann. "Don' hurt this gal! I never done nuthin'!"

As several more men crowded in behind the first, I tried to shield Mary Ann from their gaze. "Gentlemen, respect a lady's privacy!" I pleaded. "She is an innocent victim who was forced to take part in criminal activities." I had no idea whether that was true, but I wanted to protect her in any way I could.

"Beg pardon, miss," said the first witness. "We don't hold with slavery in Connecticut."

Captain Swift pushed his way through the throng, and several men tried to speak to him at once. Taking in the scene, he seemed unwilling to risk the anarchy that always threatened to erupt amongst men penned up like cattle for long periods, even when war demanded a unified will.

"Forgive the intrusion, ma'am," he said to me. "Nothing to see here, men," he lied. "Back to your duties." When his inferiors refused to move quickly enough, the Captain turned to the nearest. "Jackson!" he barked. "That's an order."

Would one man have been harder to drive away than many? It seemed as though Mary Ann and I were both safe in a crowd.

As soon as the last man had left the cabin, she dropt the neckerchief as though unwilling to touch it any longer. I impulsively threw my arms round this woman who looked like the nature-goddess of some ancient tribe. Her heat and her scent were intoxicating, together with her courage. "Woman," I told her, "you need to be properly covered."

Her warm laugh was full of innuendo. "So you say," she teased. "But you prefer me this way." I couldn't deny it.

Mary Ann's skin felt as soft as velvet, and her hands, encircling my back, felt slender and wise in their own right. She was clearly no manual laborer of the field or the kitchen. I wanted her shamelessly, regardless of what she had done.

She showed no hesitation in pressing herself against me, bosom to bosom. I was sure she had loved a woman before.

I couldn't bring her naked onto the *Black Swan*, even surrounded by the Green Men. "Hi there!" I called. "Sweeper! Someone!"

As it happened, Martin heard my call and came to the cabin door, where he stood transfixed. "Good Lord!" he said.

"Lend her your jacket, Martin," I begged. "For my sake." And so Mary Ann was wrapped in Martin's oversized jacket, which thoroughly hid her charms. She looked very odd in it, but perhaps no more so than I did when I first donned men's clothing.

THE CREW OF THE *MARTHA WASHINGTON* herded the remaining southerners off the *Dixieland*, and the prisoners offered no resistance. They undoubtedly believed that the Queen's Navy, the greatest force on the world's seas, was assisting their enemy. As I learned later, the destruction of vast southern plantations by the Union army must have caused the proudest families of the south to believe that the whole world was united to destroy them.

Whilst guarding Mary Ann from harm (as I thought), I watched the Green Men carrying as much booty as they could onto our own ship. The *Dixieland* was despoiled with shocking speed, and left to continue sinking to the bottom of the Atlantic to rest with other relics of lost civilizations.

I brought Mary Anne onto the *Black Swan*, but where was she to sleep? The captain's cabin had been crowded enough with three occupants. As Roger accompanied several of his men on their way to the hold with bales of cotton, I caught his sleeve. "Husband!" I said. "Mary Ann must be kept safe. May she and Sweeper occupy the First Mate's cabin? We have several vacancies now."

For a moment, Roger looked offended by my reference to the loss of several of his men. He may even have dreaded the prospect of having three women on board. However, he was a practical man. "Aye," he answered shortly.

I had no intention of leaving Mary Anne alone with Sweeper. "You're free now, my dear," I told her, knowing well how ambiguous a concept is freedom. "You'll be safe enough in my cabin. I'm the wife of the captain, Rodg—Captain John Greenleaf, who shares his cabin with the First Mate. Alfred must share our quarters, but he's harmless." I hoped this to be true.

"You-all have some queer notions," remarked Mary Ann.

"We outrun the law," I told her bluntly. "And so must you. Sodomy, theft and murder are all crimes in Her Majesty's Empire, and even in rebel states."

Mary Ann laughed. "Crimes for some," she agreed.

In our new quarters, I pulled out a pair of trousers and a shirt of mine for her to wear. My breath caught in my throat as she slipt Martin's jacket off her shoulders and handed it to me. She stood calmly in her bare skin, the fuzzy hair on her head half-undone from its tight plaits. That on her head matched that between her thighs. As her hands moved, her tender pink fingernails drew my gaze.

I could see at once that my clothes would not fit the woman in front of me. She was at least four inches taller than I, and although she was slim for her height, her proportions were different from mine. Her accent sounded completely and comically American, but her features spoke of Africa.

"I have nothing you can wear!" I wailed. "You shall have to stay out of sight until I can sew you a gown." I realized at once that I would have to make her clothes from whatever I could find. Raw cotton wouldn't serve until it was spun and woven. And I would have to mend our damaged sails before we could return home—if that was Roger's plan.

"Miz Emily," she said in a half-mocking tone. "Don't fret. I'll make do." She embraced me as naturally as though she had done it every day of her life. I felt completely wrapt in her musky smell, which was not at all offensive to me.

Tears stung my eyes as I returned Mary Anne's embrace. "I love a woman," I confessed. "We made vows to each other, but I lost her. I married the captain to keep up appearances."

"Uh-huh. Child, you're not the only one," she replied. "Now I'm here with you, and we can keep company."

I leant forward to press my lips to her fuller ones. A spark of energy passed from her to me like a streak of lightning. The hunger that burned in my loins felt like the symptom of a magical spell. I kissed her passionately, and she returned my fervor, but my conscience (if that is what it was) warned me not to go too far with one I hardly knew.

"Honey pie," she murmured, stroking my short hair as though she loved its smooth texture. "I won't hurt you."

I believed her. "Mary Ann, are *you* all right?"

Her look of endurance showed me that she was not suffering more than she could bear. I dreaded to imagine the sort of treatment that had been her lot. "Don't worry yourself about me, Miz Emily. I've known men before. I'm the kind of woman that keeps hold of herself no matter what. I want to taste you, and get his stink off me." She winked. "Are you going to keep your men's clothes on while I'm buck naked?"

I laughed and unbuttoned my shirt. She peeled it off my bosom, further hardening my little nubs. They felt so tender that the stroke of coarse fabric could almost make me spend. My trousers quickly followed, and I threw them into the nearest hammock to serve as a kind of cushion for our bodies.

We lay together in the tight embrace of a swinging bed intended for one. Beneath the softness of her skin I could feel a layer of hard muscle, and it comforted me. Whatever happened, she seemed capable of defending herself. As could I, of course.

I knew she was capable of killing a man. We had nothing to hide from each other.

The heat that arose from her womanly breasts carried a combined scent of salt and blood-iron. It seemed to come from the heart of the earth itself. I kissed each of her generous dark nubs, and rejoiced that she didn't push me away. I wanted to explore the mysteries of her body without reminding her of past violations. She seemed to read my thoughts.

"I want to *have* you, Captain's Lady. You're not like a boy now." My skin tingled where hers pressed against it, and my hips moved of their own accord. How I had missed the touch of a woman who reveled in the communion of female curves!

Mary Ann left burning kisses from my collarbone to each of my aching bubbies and down to my heaving ribs, my narrow waist and the valley of my navel. Liquid from my womanhood smeared my thighs. I could not honestly tell her I loved her yet, but I wanted her more than I had ever wanted anyone else. One of her capable hands slid down my belly to the opening that awaited her fingers. I could already feel the tremors that were the first phase of a full-out climax.

"Emily!" Roger's voice accompanied the sound of his fist pounding the door. "Let me in! I must speak with you."

"Hush," whispered my new lover. In an instant, she had pushed two fingers into my cunny, and was pinching my exquisitely sensitive little button of flesh. Never had I felt such ecstasy and such panic! I held my own fist against my mouth to prevent any sound from coming out as I spent and spent.

"There now," she whispered. "You needed it."

"Emily, darling! Can you answer me?" called Roger. His anxiety gave the slightest quaver to his manly baritone.

We were like a threesome in a French farce, and I could hardly prevent myself from laughing hysterically.

"One moment, Roger!" I replied, trying to emerge from the hammock with a silent economy of movement. I pulled my clothes from under Mary Ann, found a blanket and threw it over her. Buttoning my shirt as I went, I reached the cabin door in a few strides, my bare feet padding on the wooden floor. For an instant, I wondered if Mary Ann had ever crept barefooted to her master's bed.

Eight

Scorched Earth

I OPENED THE DOOR TO FIND ROGER FROWN-
ing with impatience. "Emily!" he remonstrated. "Are you
quite all right?"

"Quite," I replied, trying to appear calm whilst breathing
heavily.

"Could you possibly dress for dinner? We have been invited
to dine with Captain Swift on the *Martha Washington*, and
he has offered to accompany the *Black Swan* to a safe port.
We shall have protection from the Confederate Navy."

The captain of the union ship was undoubtedly a gentleman, but I rather wished he were not. "Roger dear, I haven't
a petticoat to my name," I told him, "and Mary Ann has no
clean clothes at all!"

Roger looked startled. "But Emily, she is only—I mean
to say, she was not invited to dine with us." He lowered his
voice. "Surely the man she killed must have friends who will
ask questions about his whereabouts, and hers. Consider our
position, dear."

To my dismay, Mary Ann had followed me and now stood
at my shoulder, draped in a blanket as though she were the
queen of an island dressed to receive an audience.

"Captain," she said with a certain hauteur. "I don't aim to
make your *position* any worse than it was when you sailed
all the way here to join the war. I am the rightful owner of

Cornford plantation near Atlanta, the richest in the state. I am Master Cornford's natural daughter and his eldest child, but usurpers took over the land when my father passed away. They sold me to a blockade-runner to further their dastardly scheme and banish me from my home."

Roger looked at her in astonishment, then looked at me. "Excuse me, Miss—" he began.

"No, excuse *me*, Captain," she continued. "Didn't you come here to help the North set all the slaves free? So you say. Now they say they believe in the Rights of Man, and they say those rights are self-evident and they come straight from God. Nobody was ever born to be a slave, that's what President Lincoln says, and his soldiers and sailors can't go against him. If the North, the United States, wins the war, do you think they will give more rights to a field hand here in the South than their own wives and daughters? If everybody has rights, that's got to include women. Even if some men don't like it, they started something and can't just stop half-way."

Mary Ann gave me and Roger the triumphant look of a Member of Parliament who has just won a debate. "Lawyers have to follow the law, and it doesn't matter if they like it or not. We have lots of lawyers here in the South, and if the North wins, I'll have rights to my land. No one could stand against me unless they break the law. For now, those northern sailors have to defend my rights until I can go to court and get the trespassers kicked off my land."

The logic of her argument seemed indisputable, but I knew that human affairs, and especially affairs of law, have rarely been based on logic. "For your sake, Mary Ann," I told her, "I hope your inheritance rights are respected."

Roger looked distressed. "Miss Cornford, you must live somewhere in the meanwhile. We're not lacking in compassion for your plight, but we can't—"

"Yes, we can," I told him. "There is room for her on the *Black Swan*."

"Captain and Miz Emily, I've got to present my case to the captain of the *Martha Washington*. It would be perfectly proper for you to introduce me as your guest."

Roger seemed unable to hide his thoughts. I could see relief in his expression, and I feared that he would offer Mary Ann to Captain Swift outright as a gift, simply to wash his hands of her. "Mary Ann," I warned her, perhaps sounding harsher than necessary, "you would not be safe on the northern ship, even if the captain accepted you. Here you have protection."

She seized my hand in a graceful gesture. "Miz Emily, I'm very grateful for your hospitality, but surely you understand my own position."

"Well then," I replied, still shaken by what I had just heard. "Are we all to dine with Captain Swift in our soiled shirts and trousers?"

"There is no need for that, Emily," my husband Roger informed me. "The Green Men are not lacking in feminine accoutrements. I'm sure we can find something which can be altered to fit each of you."

Presently Roger strode about the ship, accosting members of his crew who had cherished gowns, stockings and crinolines on board. As it happened, Hopwell (the man Sweeper had wounded a fortnight before) was of a height with Mary Ann, and he had a gown of blue *peau de soie* which suited her well after she had cleverly made it smaller at the waist. Hopwell was improving steadily in health, but was still convalescing and therefore unable to take part in "drag" soirees with the rest of the crew. Although he clearly resented having to give up one of his favorite possessions, he had no reason to refuse a request from his captain.

Dujour the cook had a rose-colored gown that he had made for himself. He offered it to me with his best wishes, and even tugged and smoothed the fabric when I tried it on, and pinned the seams that needed to be taken in.

Mary Ann and I helped each other with our preparations, and tried to make haste. I lent her a ribbon which she arranged into the semblance of a flower to wear in her bushy hair after she had let it out of its plaits and combed it with her fingers. My own hair had grown since its last cutting, but it was still too short to form a chignon, so I fashioned a snood out of fabric from the hem of my gown and used it to cover as much of my hair as possible.

The results of our efforts were less than ideal. We agreed to forego crinolines under the circumstances, and we hoped that our skirts would hide my unsuitable men's shoes and Mary Ann's bare feet. She didn't seem at all discomfited by her lack of shoe leather.

Touching her and receiving her touches aroused me thoroughly, but there was no time for us to make love. As soon as we were presentable, we approached Roger and Martin, who each took one of us by the arm and steadied us as we made our way from one ship to the other. The difficulty of any activity, even simple movement, whilst dressed in lady-like attire made me wonder how I could have worn corsets and petticoats so willingly before I boarded the *Black Swan*. Ships in general were not built to accommodate ladies.

THE *MARTHA WASHINGTON* WAS OUTFITTED with every modern convenience, and gave an impression of polished wood and gleaming metal. We were escorted to the mess hall where the captain and his officers awaited us. If any of the men had reservations about allowing women onto their ship, our appearance apparently changed their feelings completely.

All the men stood as we were escorted to our places at table, and I could see that several cocks were also standing in too-snug blue trousers. The excitement in the room was as palpable as tension in the air before a storm.

"Welcome, welcome, ladies and gentlemen!" exclaimed Patrick Mulligan, First Mate. Captain Swift clapped his hands together, and applause spread round the table. The sound echoed off the walls.

A vision of naked men burst onto my mind's-eye. As clearly as though it were actually happening, I saw Mary Ann spread on her back on the linen tablecloth, her skirts above her waist, as a laughing man prepared to mount her. I felt the wooden table under my own backside as another man spread my knees apart. I could see several men mock-punching each other and observing each other's red, swollen pricks with obvious interest as they awaited their turn at our cunnies.

Despite my alarm, I felt a rush of warmth between my legs. As fervently as I hoped to be spared the humiliation of ravishment by a whole ship's crew, I wondered if I could control my reactions if I were to be seized against my will, exposed and plundered by members of the Union Navy.

I wondered whether the surviving men of the *Dixieland* were shackled in the hold. I strained to hear groans or the clank of chains, but I heard only the ordinary bustle of mealtime on a ship.

In the mess hall, there was a round of introductions, and an initial course of polite, inconsequential remarks. Dishes were brought to the table. "Let us give thanks," said Captain Swift. He folded his hands and bowed his head, and whilst everyone else at the table followed suit, he prayed aloud at some length to the generous God who had provided both sustenance and a military advantage to the Yankee cause.

We all busied ourselves filling our plates. The man seated next to me, the ship's medical officer (a man known as "Bones") asked me so assiduously whether I wanted more that I wished he would stop drawing attention to me. I had not realized how hungry I was whilst surviving on the unappetizing fare we had with us on the *Black Swan*. Here was fish, cured beef, soup, preserved vegetables, bread and pudding, with our choice of whisky, rum or tea to wet our throats. I tried not to appear greedy.

Roger asked Captain Swift what he knew of the progress of the war. "Victory is certain," responded the American. Yet his demeanor was subdued. "Strategies have been employed which I would not describe in the presence of the gentler sex. You, sirs, must understand the necessity for extreme measures in a war."

Roger nodded in agreement. Martin looked uncomfortable.

"War is no longer a sport for gentlemen," the captain explained, as though thinking aloud. "I doubt that it ever was, in reality. This war has torn our strong young nation apart and robbed us of our innocence. Yet we do what we must for the greater good."

"Captain, you need not excuse yourself for destroying a corrupt society," said Mary Ann. "The prosperity of the southern states is built on forced labor."

"Indeed, my dear," replied the captain, studying her décolletage. "The Union intends to abolish slavery and all the evils attendant upon it."

"We prefer our women willing," said Bones. He drew back his lips in a smile that showed most of his large teeth. A suggestive laugh spread from man to man.

Roger half-rose from his seat. "I brought my wife here in trust that she and our lady friend would be treated with respect, sir," he said.

"Oh, you don't have to defend my honor, Captain," Mary Ann interjected. "I'm familiar with the ways of men. Northern, southern, black, brown, white or yellow, they're all alike under their clothes. There's no harm in honest desire, and no sucha thing as an unnatural vice. God made us the way we are. Don't you-all agree?"

Patrick was already on his feet. He strode to Mary Ann's chair, stood behind her, and slid his hands down over her shoulders to cup her breasts. "You're a fine wench, my dear," he told her, making the adjective sound like "foin."

The sound of men's breathing was audible. In a moment, I thought, the officers would tear off their uniforms, sweep dishes to the floor, lay us on the table, and surge into us like ocean waves.

Mary Ann pulled Patrick's hands off her bubbies, which shook with her effort. "I need a favor from you, man," she said. "Before you take any more liberties, listen to me seriously. I need help to secure my inheritance."

As the First Mate hovered over her, Mary Ann addressed her plea to Captain Swift. She explained to him, as she had to Roger and me, that she was the rightful mistress of Cornford plantation, and needed the government of the Union to support her claim.

Bones covered his mouth with his sleeve to smother a laugh, and instead snorted like a hog. His astonished merriment seemed contagious, and soon all the men were bursting with it. The delirium lasted for a moment, and then subsided into silence.

"Miss Mary Ann," the First Mate addressed her tenderly, "even now, General Sherman is marching through Georgia. Please forgive me for bearing bad news, but you must not go there if you value your life."

"The Union army intends to scour the land," added Captain Swift. "The very earth will be scorched, and all the inhabitants driven off."

"Good Lord!" exclaimed Martin before he could bridle his tongue. No one needed to explain to us that "driven off" was most likely an evasive term for wholesale murder.

"Not a shed nor a mule nor a crop will be left from Atlanta to the sea," said another man, who seemed to believe that further explanation was necessary. "Georgia will be left as barren as the Sahara Desert."

The look of horror on Mary Ann's expressive face showed that she could imagine too well the destruction of the farm she still thought of as her home. "I don't know what you learned in school up North," she spat. "Only the Devil and all his fiends would do such a thing." Had General Sherman been present, Mary Ann would probably have challenged him to a duel.

Captain Swift remained calm but unsympathetic. "My dear, I would have preferred to avoid this discussion, but your ill-advised request has forced us to tell you in the bluntest terms what must be done to reunite our nation."

"The rebellion of the South comes from those who outfit the army and work the land with captive labor," another man pointed out. "The rebels have too many fox-holes where they can hide. We must—um—dig them out." He was looking intently at Mary Ann.

Bones looked impatient. "Gentlemen!" he addressed them. "Is this gathering not dedicated to pleasure? Our dusky guest has told us how well she accepts the nature of men, and I can see that Mrs. Greenleaf is a woman of the same type, if you'll pardon the expression. We have fed our gullets, but our other parts have not yet been satisfied." The man placed a large hand over the mound at his crotch and smiled mean-ingfully at all his fellow-officers.

Was he too much in his cups to know what he was say-ing? Had the Yankee captain invited my husband to bring his women to a Roman orgy, and had Roger been too long away from regular military men to understand? Had the condi-tion of our ship made our hosts skeptical of our claim to be emissaries of Her Majesty's Navy?

I glanced at Roger, then at red-faced Martin, who tugged at his collar. Both of them rose to the occasion by standing upright. "Gentlemen," said Roger, allowing a slight sarcas-tic drawl to undermine the designation. "We brought you the good will of our Queen and our assistance in catching Confederate criminals who defy your blockade. We abhor slavery as much as you profess to do, and we have saved this good lady from its shackles. Our God expects no less of us."

Martin looked surprised by Roger's unexpected burst of piety, but he seemed equally determined to speak his mind. "We are civilized men," he said, "and we enjoy—er, accept the company of women. We can assure you they aren't whores. Not that we'd mind."

"We must take our leave," I told Roger, *sotto voce.*

"Now we shall take our leave," he told Captain Swift, "before further misunderstandings ensue. We thank you for an excellent meal. We hope that the government of Great Britain and her Empire shall never have occasion to regret forming an alliance with the United States."

"No regrets," said one of the men, nodding as though in time to a jig that only he could hear.

"If this war isn't no sport for gentlemen," sneered Mary Ann, "per-*haps* that's because no gentlemen signed up for it."

I could feel my heart beating beneath my ribs as I stood up. Mary Ann was already standing on her durable feet. To my great relief, the Americans made no move to prevent us from leaving their premises.

"The night is still young," said Mr. Mulligan, "and we would enjoy more of your company, but if you must leave us, you must. We intend no offense to your delicate sensibilities." This speech carried an undertone of rude irony, but I refused to let it linger in my mind. I wanted only to make my way back to the *Black Swan* without tumbling into the ocean, or onto a slippery deck with my legs in the air.

"Farewell, friends," said Captain Swift as though he were truly a gracious host. "And fair sailing."

Nine

Terms of Occupation

THE NIGHT WAS CLEAR, AND THE LIGHT OF the moon and the stars poured down upon us like a blessing, enabling us to find our way back to the deck of our ship without mishap. A wave of homesickness washed over me as I wondered whether my parents and my brothers and sisters were watching the same sky from their home in London, and hoping the war in America would end quickly.

Mary Ann moved like a woman carrying a heavy burden. I wanted to lift her spirits and to feel the heat of her body pressed to mine. "Lover," I said, wrapping an arm about her waist, "please don't lose hope. When one door closes, another one opens."

"Gal," she sighed, "you're sweeter than sugar, but you can't help me. I've lost everything I had in the world." Her dark eyes shone with tears. She looked gravely into mine. "Unless we can stop the Yankees."

"Mary Ann, you can't stop an army! Even the Green Men can't do that." Amazed as I was at her stubborn refusal to acknowledge her powerless situation, I couldn't help comparing her favorably to Lucy. *Sometimes,* I thought, *it's better for a woman to cling to an outrageous dream than to compromise her soul in the name of necessity.*

"I bet your Queen doesn't know that Union army she likes so much is planning to burn up the whole South." Mary Ann had a mad gleam of hope in her eyes. "She could stop them all right. And I know she believes in women's right to inherit land and social position. She's got to, considering who she is. Miz Emily, if you help me write a letter to Her Royal Majesty, or whatever she's supposed to be called, maybe we can send it by a passing clipper and hope it gets to her palace in time."

I was tempted to hoot with laughter. It seemed that even an American could cherish a vain hope of making the Queen's acquaintance. I pulled Mary Ann to me for a gentle kiss that became passionate as she responded. I wanted to protect her from her own foolishness, but I couldn't bear to break her heart.

At length, I withdrew from her full, warm lips to look into the depths of her eyes. "Mary Ann," I told her, "you must listen to me seriously. The Queen will not help either side in this wretched American war, and she would have no more sympathy for your plight than Queen Bess had for Mary Queen of Scots in exile. And the men who write the laws of all the countries on earth would condemn everyone on this ship. We have no one to rely on but each other."

She opened her mouth to speak, but I pressed two fingers against her lips. "Woman," I said, "it's no good trying to think your way out of a maze when your blood is up. Did you think those men on the Yankee ship would ravish you?" I rudely grabbed one of her breasts as though I were a drunken sailor.

Mary Ann laughed and twisted away, pulling my hand behind my back. "They sure enough wanted to. There wasn't a gentleman on that ship, and they were all looking at you with the devil in their eyes, too, gal."

"Were you frightened?" When I thought she wasn't expecting it, I brought my knee up between her legs, where her delicious quim was hidden behind folds of blue *peau de soie*.

She deftly reached for my bent knee within its own casing of fabric, and almost pulled me off my feet. "No such thing, but I was disappointed." She grinned at me in explanation. "The First Mate looked like he was willing to reach an understanding with me, and I thought we could all dance a fine jig to help each other out. Men won't do something for nothing."

Unreasonable jealousy surged through my veins and heated my face. I pulled the bodice of her borrowed gown, popping several buttons in back. "Do you offer yourself to anyone who can help you, then?"

Mary Ann pushed me away, but she kept her full strength in reserve. "Who's asking me?" she retorted. "I'll do what I have to do to get what's mine, but I wouldn't promise what I don't mean."

"What if those Yankees had offered to keep you, and take you back to your plantation?" I replied. I pushed her toward the cabin I thought of as our bridal chamber. "Would you let them all do this?" I plunged my hands under her skirt and roughly seized her buttocks with both hands.

Her arse-muscles flexed as though they had a will of their own. "Miz Captain," she sneered. "How many babies do you think he'll get on you? You're a good wife, aren't you?" She grabbed my hair to pull my head back. She kissed me like a drunken sailor as my coiffure went to ruin.

We wrestled each other into the empty cabin, where she pushed me into the hammock and fell atop me. "Do you think I'm your servant?" she demanded. "Do y'all think I want to go to England and raise your young 'uns?"

I had not imagined Mary Ann as a nanny, nor myself as a mother. "You fool," I responded before I could soften my words. "He loves Martin."

She lifted my skirt above my waist and used the fabric as a cushion on which to rest. Her fingers sought out my slit, and my wetness made her mission damnably easy. "You're a bigger fool," she declared, her lips so close to mine that I could see them glisten in the dim light. "You're Captain's wife. He can claim his rights any time he wants, gal. He can share you with his First Mate, too. Maybe you'd like that." She eased one finger, then another into my quim, and I welcomed her despite my best intentions to resist.

Mary Ann pressed her breasts against mine, and I could feel her heartbeat through the thin fabric that barely separated my skin from hers. Her tormenting fingers inside me were replaced by something cold, smooth and hard. I yelped like an excited terrier, and she pressed a warm, dewy hand against my mouth. "Hush," she ordered. "It's a spoon from the Yankee ship. A souvenir to remember me by."

I couldn't puzzle out her meaning whilst her silver instrument stroked my little button without mercy, and her fingers returned to claim my cunt. Just as I was on the brink of climax, she wriggled her whole body violently downwards, threatening to pitch us both out of the hammock. "This is mine tonight," she said, as though to explain her coarse (even piratical) behavior. I knew which part of me she was so bent on claiming. She pushed my skirt out of her way with both hands, and spread it over my head like a tent.

Mary Ann fastened her hot mouth on my slit. Her tongue burrowed between my lower lips and her teeth nibbled on my little man-in-a-boat, which felt greatly swollen from her earlier attention. I felt as though I could burst apart into a thousand streaks of light, like fireworks in the night sky. I held her head of dear, woolly hair for comfort as I spent and spent.

Mary Ann uncovered my face and kissed me tenderly. Her dark eyes seemed as liquid as brimming pools. In that moment, I could forgive her for anything, but I couldn't be sure she felt the same way about me. "Darling," I sighed. "Does it really trouble you so much that Roger and I have an arrangement?"

She laughed softly and bitterly. "You have a marriage, missus. That's your *arrangement* with the captain of this creaky old pirate ship full of men with their own petticoats. Where's there a place for me?"

I surmised that Mary Ann didn't want a position as a crew-member of the *Black Swan*. It came to me that she wanted recognition and respect, like everyone else in the world. If she could never become mistress of her own plantation, at the very least, she wanted to see herself reflected in my eyes as a lady in the feudal sense.

"Mary Ann, dearest," I replied, "there's a place for you in my heart. I will call you by your real name if you prefer it, and if you'll teach it to me. I'm willing to practice until I say it properly. I will never let you come to harm if I can help it. You'll see. And Roger respects you as I respect his lover Martin."

She lay her head between my breasts, holding me tightly in her arms. "Honey," she sighed, "I've been answering to Mary Ann all my life, and these here Green Men would never rec-ollect the African name my mama gave me even if they could get their tongues around it. I can teach it to you in private, but I have to keep on being Mary Ann everywhere else." She lifted her head to gaze at me with her expressive eyes. "You put a spell on me, Emily. That's a misfortune for women like us. We've got to be hard as rocks, and not let soft feelings get in our way."

I held her with all my strength. "Love could make us strong-er, dear," I told her. "It doesn't have to weaken us."

Mary Ann looked thoughtful. "I want to see you all over, every inch of your pearly skin. I want to know you're mine, honey. Ladies' clothes are a waste of good cloth." She reached behind me and pulled the sides of my bodice apart, popping buttons. She ripped a seam in her eagerness to slide the long sleeves off my arms.

We proceeded to pull, tug and unbutton each other's gowns, and to free ourselves from a rumpled lake of fabric. When my hardened nipples were exposed to her sight, Mary Ann fell on them like a starving shipwreck survivor discovering ripe fruit. She closed her eyes and drew each nipple in turn into the heat of her mouth. As she squeezed my bubbies with her hands, she suckled me until I thought I would go mad.

What must a baby's mouth feel like on a mother's milk-filled teat? The thought almost shocked me out of my pleasure-trance. Could a human mother be so like a hog that sinks into bliss when feeding her young? Well, why not? The most pious churchmen say we are all God's creatures.

I knew I would climax if Mary Ann continued much longer. At the right moment, she reached down to tickle my wet slit, and I spent on her fingers.

I breathed deeply, even though the air in our cabin was far from fresh. "Mary Ann," I murmured. "I love your touch. Please don't misunderstand me. I know you have loved a woman before, and I don't mind. Let's not keep secrets from each other."

"Oh, gal, both of us can tell each other some stories," she laughed. There would be time for Story Hour after I had satisfied her current need.

I wrapt my arms about Mary Ann's shoulders, and raised my head to press my lips to hers. She seemed to melt in my embrace. The musk from all her warm, hidden places smelt like perfume to me. I teased her nipples until they changed their shape and texture whilst she squirmed and sighed.

Her back felt as satin-smooth as a calm sea when I stroked its length, and slid down to grasp her two beautiful, round arse-cheeks. "Has anyone had you here?" I asked, pushing the tip of one finger against her puckered opening. She hesitated a moment too long, and thus answered my question.

"Easy, gal," she warned me. "Down there's not much used to visitors."

I coaxed her tiny hole to open by moving my finger in small spirals, and resolved to use butter or oil to ease my way on a future occasion. For the meanwhile, I explored the hammock with my free hand, but could not find the stolen spoon. I had no recourse but to seek out her cunt with my fingers alone.

The woman had been aroused for most of the evening and had shown devilish cunning in prompting my own surrender. Not wanting to be outdone, I pushed two and then three fingers into her. Finding it impossible to give equal attention to both her openings, I withdrew from her arse and surged in and out of her cunt with merciless strokes.

There was a sound of footsteps nearby, but I could not afford to investigate the presence of a spirit or a flesh-and-blood intruder. Mary Ann seemed oblivious to all except our wild dance in the swinging hammock. "Uh!" she gasped in surprise or alarm. "Take—care, honey."

"Sweeper!" I shouted too late, seeing her standing over us. Sweeper—or Alfred—was holding some shiny object which disappeared between Mary Ann's lower cheeks. The victim of this trespass clenched my fingers with her inner muscles in paroxysms of transport, and soaked the hammock with her juice.

In an instant, Mary Ann had recovered from her ecstasy. She bounded out of the hammock and seized Alfred by the throat. "What the devil are you doing?" demanded my lover. Although Alfred was fully clothed and Mary Ann wore only her tawny skin, the outraged woman had the advantage.

Alfred choked and squawked, and I could see Mary Ann pressing a metal object against her throat whilst holding her against the wall of the cabin with the force of a shoulder and a knee.

"Cap'n—gave me—this cabin!" explained Alfred as soon as Mary Ann allowed her a much-needed breath.

"That doesn't mean—" I began. What a dreadful mess had I created by asking Roger to let Mary Ann share quarters with Alfred? This was all my doing.

"Look here!" exclaimed Mary Ann. "I don't care what Captain told you. Nobody touches me if I don't say so, do you hear me?"

"Beg pardon, Miss," muttered Alfred between coughs. "You looked too invitin'."

I managed to stand on shaking legs. "Mary Ann, Alfred, I'm so sorry. Please forgive me." I turned to Mary Ann, and her blazing eyes offered little hope of forgiveness. "I asked Roger if Alfred could stay here with you. I couldn't tell Roger exactly how things were between us, could I?"

"If you don't," threatened the proud beauty, "I will."

"Wot's this then?" demanded Alfred, looking from one of us to the other.

"Peace, women!" I begged. "We can't afford hostilities amongst ourselves when we're in such perilous straits."

"*Wim*-men?" asked Mary Ann, her voice swooping.

"I'll explain everything," I promised. "Mary Ann, Alfred is as female as we are."

"Am not!" protested the bosun.

Mary Ann snickered. "Show us the evidence," she teased. Alfred's eyes flashed fire, but she limited herself to folding her arms firmly across her chest.

"Excuse me," I apologized to both. "Alfred is a man in spirit. Mary Ann, she—he—was very kind to me on the long voyage."

"You kept company," Mary Ann corrected me. "Y'all were like two catfish in a pond full of water moccasins."

The exact meaning of her simile eluded me, but I was relieved to think that at last Mary Ann understood my relationship with the Green Men. I felt obliged to correct all other misunderstandings, if possible. "He—Alfred—only loves one person, and that someone does not return those feelings. Mary Ann, whatever you think of Alfred here, sh-he deserves our sympathy." Before I could stop myself, I blurted, "Alfred would die for Captain Roger."

Alfred sputtered and turned red just as someone knocked on the cabin door. "Emily?" Roger's concerned baritone was unmistakable. "Is everything all right? I couldn't help hearing—raised voices."

"We're doing splendidly, Roger," I called out, "like three birds in a nest."

"May I come in?" he asked. The question was merely a formality, and he didn't wait for an answer. I snatched up my gown and wrapped it about me. Mary Ann's parallel motions looked like a parody of maidenly modesty.

"Ladies, it's rather late," Roger explained awkwardly. "Emily, would you—I mean to say, there is room for one more in my cabin. There is no need to quarrel over sleeping arrangements." His eyes rested gently on Alfred, and then I knew that Roger had overheard my indiscreet remark.

I pressed the point. "Roger, husband, I know you to be generous. If you and Martin could find room for Alfred, I'm sure sh-he would be grateful." I looked at Alfred, and he—as I resolved to think of him—seemed too mortified to speak. I continued on his behalf: "A little attention would comfort him immensely, Roger, and I'm sure he won't overstay his welcome once you explain your terms."

Mary Ann laughed openly. Roger looked at Alfred as though seeing him for the first time, and there was much kindness in his gaze. "How thoughtful of you, Emily," he responded. "Alfred, me lad, would you care to join me and my First Mate in our cabin?"

Alfred found his voice. "Aye, with all my heart, Sir."

"Adieu, ladies," said Roger. "Sleep well."

Alone with Mary Ann in our hammock, I struggled to explain my unusual marriage. "Whatever anyone might say about Roger, dear, he is no worse than any other rogue who calls himself a gentleman. He is much better than a husband. He's a friend."

"P'raps," she answered. "But if Alfred tries to use a screw-handle on Captain the way he used it on me, I bet he'll clarify his *terms* right quick."

Laughing in each other's arms, lying in our pungent fluids, we fell into a sleep as deep as the ocean that carried us. Our future was unclear, but for now we were at rest.

Ten

A Distracting Tale, Part One

THE FOLLOWING DAY DAWNED CLEAR AND calm—almost too much so, as there was barely enough wind to ripple our sails. We were beyond sight of land. As far as I knew, we had no destination and no way to replace our dwindling supplies until we could reach a port where our cotton and tobacco would be so welcome that no one would ask how they came into our possession.

Some of the men had fashioned a net which they cast overboard each day in the hope of catching dinner before some denizen of the deep would render the net useless by tearing holes in it. And I would mend the net, once again, so that everyone on board might be supplied with enough fish to do a day's work. Self-pity, bred from monotonous routine, sometimes prompted me to imagine us all as damned souls in Hell.

I thought of continuing my fantasy story about the warrior queen and her army of Amazons so that I could share it with Mary Ann. However, that story seemed to come from another time in my life, before the complications of an actual war had intruded into my imagination.

"Roger," I asked as he stood at the rail, gazing at the trackless water. "What do you plan to do?"

"Sail to Nassau," he answered.

"To live?" I had asked him this before, and his answer had not been certain.

"Oh, Emily," he groaned. I noticed the dark shadows under his eyes, and guessed that he had not slept well. "I can't bear to think that I may never see England again. For now, we need to trade some of our cargo for the necessities of life. That shall be our first order of business. After that, we must consider the possibilities."

I imagined a noose hanging over the head of every man on board who dared to dream of home, yet homesickness was almost visible as a general malaise. I knew that Roger had never given up hope of making peace with Society and claiming his inheritance. Had he really wanted to live and die as a pirate, he would never have married me. And had Lucy not broken my heart, I would never have accepted him. A fine pair of swashbucklers we were.

Mary Ann showed more strength of resolve than Roger or Martin or I, but her home was probably being burnt to ashes as our ship drifted in the watery wilderness. Her possibilities were bleaker than ours. And Alfred seemed to be the most dispossessed of us all.

As though summoned by my thought, Alfred and Martin approached arm-in-arm. Whatever had transpired amongst the three in the captain's cabin, it had made at least two of them more amiable.

"Good morning, Sir," said Alfred to Roger, and his words had a musical cadence. Indeed, Alfred carried his hand-carved flute, and seemed disposed to play a serenade to his two cabin-mates on it. Sea-birds circling overhead cawed like jeering boys, as though daring Alfred to join their chorus.

Mary Ann joined our little party and kissed me heartily in sight of the rest. I responded without demur, knowing that none of the witnesses had a right to protest. We all wore working-men's shirts and trousers, and this style of dress had come to be accepted by everyone in our little world, regardless of rank or gender.

"We're headed to Nassau," I informed her, gesturing to starboard.

"There's a storm coming from that way, honey," she warned. "Look at the birds. We'll need to take cover."

Like a fickle goddess, the sky changed its mood within minutes. Lavender-gray clouds rolled in from the horizon, and a breeze sprang up to harry the waves. My internal weather seemed just as unsettled, but I could not be sure whether my courses were coming on or whether my body were reacting to the inadequacy of breakfast, or to nature's dyspepsia—or all together.

Roger announced that he and Martin would stand watch. He encouraged Mary Ann, Alfred and me to take shelter in the captain's cabin, which afforded more room than the one I shared with Mary Ann. "More experienced men can man the sails," said Roger. "Forgive me, my dears, but amateurs on deck would be more of a liability than we can afford." I realized that whilst I had learnt to handle a sword, I had neglected to pay sufficient attention to the sail-craft that was so necessary to our progress. As galling as my ignorance felt, Roger was right.

THE MOTION OF THE SHIP HAD INCREASED by the time we settled ourselves. "Tale-telling is a fine way to pass the time," I told my companions. *And to distract ourselves from fear and discomfort,* I thought. "I propose that we tell each other our histories, or as much as we choose to disclose. Mary Ann, will you begin?"

"Most gladly, Miz Emily," she replied. "Now y'all know I was born and raised on Cornford plantation, the pride of Georgia. You prob'ly never guessed how much contentment we had there, even the ones in the slave cabins behind the big house."

"I thank my stars we got no slavery in England," Alfred declared with patriotic fervor.

"What you got prob'ly isn't much better," she retorted. "Y'all have to bow and curtsey to a whole bunch of royalty and mucky-mucks who're no better than the common people, if truth be told. Some are like to be a sight worse. But if you please, I'll continue the thread of my narrative." Alfred and I encouraged her to go on.

"My mama's name was Irikosima, given to her by her mama, but she was called Miz Grace. She was born a slave, but my father freed her after he fell in love with her. He was a white man, Master of Cornford, and she was as dark and beautiful as fine mahogany, from the real African stock. Unions like theirs happened more often than some white folks like to believe—or colored folks either.

"My mama sat at the table in the big house with my daddy every evening at dinner, and he didn't care who knew it. She slept in his bed and kept her clothes in her own dressing-room. She had a silk ball-gown, a corset from France, and a gold promise ring from him."

"If he freed her," asked Alfred, "why couldn't she leave?"

"She loved him," Mary Ann retorted as though to an idiot. "They lived together as husband and wife for fourteen years, and I never heard a cross word between the two of them except when Daddy walked into the parlor in his muddy boots.

"I used to watch them dancing together while Sophy, our housekeeper, played a Viennese waltz on the pianoforte. They both loved to dance, and my father knew all the steps. He was more of a gentleman than any of these jumped-up planters who think they can run a plantation just because they win enough money from gambling to buy a few acres of land."

Mary Ann paused to wipe both her eyes. I held her nearest hand and squeezed it. "My dear," I said, "I hope you had a happy childhood."

"Happy enough," she replied, "but we were always so much by ourselves when Mama was alive. She named me Ekineba, and Daddy named me Mary Ann, so I had two names like her, not that many folks were inclined to call me anything respectful. All the other families in the county just cut my parents dead after they came calling one time. It was okay for all those masters to rape their slave women, but not for my father to introduce my mother as his hostess, the mistress of Cornford."

I wondered how many Englishmen, even the staunchest defenders of liberty and universal rights, would love and marry an African woman, or even a mulatto. I had never heard of such a thing in Jamaica. But if I could feel as entranced by Mary Ann as I did, perhaps the color bar was based only on the natural feelings of white men, and not all of them at that. I would simply have to decide for myself which "truths" passed the test of experience.

Mary Ann continued: "My father wanted to do the right thing and marry my mother, especially after I was born, but no minister would do the job. And they call themselves Christians! One day after church, Mama and Daddy said wedding vows to each other in the parlor, and I was their witness and Maid of Honor. Mama made everybody take their shoes off in honor of the occasion, and Sophy played the wedding march. Daddy gave Mama a ring and he said they were married in their hearts, but it wasn't legal. After that, he always told me if anyone called me illegitimate, I should tell them to talk to Master Cornford about that, and he would confirm me as his natural daughter and the apple of his eye."

By now, Mary Ann's eyes were brimming with tears. I helped her wipe her eyes on a tail of my shirt, having no handkerchief. Even Alfred seemed to be moved. "There, there, dear," he said to Mary Ann, but she turned away from him to nestle in my arms. Alfred was not yet in her good graces.

"My father didn't want to tell us how worried he was," she went on, "but I know some hoodlums threatened to burn us out of house and home just like the Union army. He never let Mama or me go any place alone without him or Sam, our driver. It near drove me stir-crazy, never going for a walk without a chaperone." The storyteller sighed and rolled her eyes heavenwards.

"I always wanted brothers and sisters," she told us. "I thought we could have so much fun together! From time to time, I saw Mama in the family way, but she always lost the baby. Sometimes the midwife came and stayed for a long time, but then Daddy always told me my little brother or sister went to heaven so we could have an angel watching over us. I didn't know why they never wanted to stay with us and grow up at Cornford!

"I think my mama was in delicate health when she was having babies, but now I think a few other things too. Nobody really liked our little family. Even some of the household staff thought Mama had jumped up too high. They didn't see a reason for me to grow up in the big house instead of in the slave quarters with the other pickaninnies. And I don't know where my father found midwives, or how well he knew them."

Mary Ann looked ominously at me and at Alfred. "There's a lot of gris-gris in the South," she told us, "a lot of root-workers who can cure you or kill you with poison. I think someone was plotting against us, but it was no use saying that to my father. He said it was all just leftover superstition in the Age of Science." Her tears started afresh. "My mama died of childbed fever when I was thirteen. I was just turning a young lady, and I needed her more than ever, but she was gone. Our house felt so empty after that! I had my own boudoir, and I just stayed there like a hermit in a cave until Daddy brought Miz Rosamund home."

"Your new mum?" asked Alfred.

Mary Ann snorted. "She wasn't ever a mother to me. She came from up North, and Daddy courted her for two years before she got him to marry her. She was the spindliest woman I ever did see, with no lips and no bosom. She and my daddy invited people to the house all the time. I didn't want to make trouble, so I just stayed out of their way."

I wrapt an arm about the storyteller's waist. "Didn't you go to school?" I asked.

"Of course," she retorted. "I attended Miz Brightman's Day School for Free Colored Girls. I learned Household Management, Cooking, Sewing, Hairdressing, Deportment, French, and Elocution. For my senior recitation, I chose Shakespeare: 'When in disgrace with fortune and men's eyes/I all alone beweep my outcast state.' The teacher said I had a flair for dramatic presentations."

Alfred seemed as captivated by Mary Ann's history as though it were the *Tales of the Arabian Nights*. "Cor!" said Alfred. "Me dad wouldn't let me go to school. He said me eldest brother could think for all of us. When I said I wanted to learn how to think for meself, he gave me a thrashin' so me brothers and sisters wouldn't get any such notions." Alfred thought of something else. "Din't you have any friends, then?"

Mary Ann gave us both a knowing look. "I had friends and then I had Charley."

"Your school friend?" Just asking this question gave me a pang.

"No such thing," she explained. "Charley was how Miz Charlotte liked to be called, and she wasn't colored, exactly, though she was kind of a dark for a white woman. Rosamund said Charley was her niece."

"Oho," said Alfred.

"Miz Rosamund couldn't very well say she had a love-child of her own if she wanted all the white folks in the county to think she was such a lady. She said Charley's parents were both dead, but Charley couldn't recall any besides her."

"Tell us all," I prompted the storyteller.

"Charley was"—Mary Ann sighed—"like nobody else I knew. She was two years older than me, and she found work as a live-in companion to old Miz Forrester. She was really a nursemaid, but she never complained. Charley didn't want to live with Miz Rosamund any more than Miz Rosamund wanted her tagging along once she'd set her sights on my father.

"Charley was strong as a man, and she knew how to shoot and fish and ride a horse like a member of the cavalry. She had no patience for womanly arts like dressmaking or arranging hair or dancing a Virginia Reel. She said she was too clumsy, but I didn't find her so."

"Aha." I pulled Mary Ann into my arms and kissed her. "I can guess how you discovered that."

Mary Ann chuckled after our kiss had ended. "Then I don't have to explain it to y'all," she replied. "She had a way about her. Charley was never a dainty little thing. Miz Rosamund said she needed to improve herself a lot to find a husband, but I liked her better the way she was.

"Charley showed me how to bait a hook and catch a fish, then fry it in corn meal right over an open fire. I never tasted anything so good! I always liked having some useful skills so I wouldn't have to depend on others once I was a grown woman. She also showed me how to fight off any man that might try to take liberties, and that is the most useful skill a colored woman can have."

Alfred looked away from her. May Ann looked at me, and she seemed to guess what I wanted to know.

"It started," resumed the storyteller, gazing modestly at her hands, "when I asked her if she ever had a beau up North. She said yes, but he wasn't exactly her first choice. She said she would rather court a young lady like me. I knew my father wouldn't like that, and my teachers at school would tell me to resist the Devil, but I never met a boy I liked as much as Charley."

Mary Ann glanced at me in such a comical way that I almost laughed aloud. "I hope you don't mind, honey," she pleaded.

"Not at all," I assured her. "It's only natural." Alfred's agreement glowed in his eyes.

"I spent a lot of time with Charley at Miz Forrester's house. The old lady was so blind we could kiss and cuddle in her own parlor, and she thought I was helping Charley with her cross-stitch." Mary Ann laughed at the memory. "That was before Miz Rosamund threatened to put her in the insane asylum."

At that moment, the ship lurched so violently that we were all thrown against the wall. I feared for our lives. What must Roger and Martin be enduring in the face of the gale? Was Mary Ann's tale to be cut short by worse events in the present?

To my relief, Roger opened the cabin door to offer us a news bulletin. He was drenched in seawater like a triton, but he showed no distress; fighting the elements seemed to have awakened his natural courage. Martin followed him, blinking as drops fell persistently from his hair into his eyes. "Ladies," said Roger, "we must ride out the storm. We shall be in the First Mate's cabin temporarily."

I did not ask how my husband and his dear companion intended to comfort each other in the face of the ocean's wrath. Considering our possible fate, I felt overwhelmed with love for all my ship-mates. "Alfred and Mary Ann," I told them, "if we don't survive to see the next dawn, I could not have better company in the hereafter."

"We're not going to die," Mary Ann informed me. "I'd feel it in my bones. We just need to keep our spirits up." Toward that end, she wrapt her arms round both of us, and it seemed that she had forgiven Alfred for his impudence.

I revelled in the warmth and even the tangy aroma of our three bodies. I hoped this tableau was a harbinger of better days to come because I was not prepared to meet Davy Jones just yet.

Eleven

A Distracting Tale, Part Two

AT LAST, THE OCEAN SEEMED TO CALM herself, and the motion of the ship grew more regular. My inwards settled enough that I became aware of the pangs of hunger which told me better than the most accurate watch how much time had passed since we last ate. I knew that we all needed a diversion.

"Mary Ann, my dear, you left us in suspense. Would you tell us what happened next?"

"Yes, tell us," said Alfred politely.

"Where did I leave off? Oh yes," she remembered aloud, "what they did to cure me, and Charley. We should have known we couldn't carry on the way we did without anybody trying to stop us. We didn't see what was coming next." I felt for Mary Ann and her lost love, but I was glad the upheavals of her life had thrown her into my arms.

She continued: "Miz Rosamund never thought I was fit company for Charley, and she often spoke to her about it. Charley liked to speak her mind, and I'm sure she said more than she should have. That's how Miz Rosamund got the notion that we shared an unnatural vice. Masturbation is what she called it. I don't think my father would have thought any such thing about me if Miz Rosamund hadn't gotten him worked up. She said all that unladylike stuff Charley liked was the direct result of going insane from too much self-stimulation. It sure worried Daddy." Mary Ann twisted her hands together.

"They were ignorant fools," I remarked.

"P'raps, Emily, but all the preachers and doctors and leaders of society were on their side. My daddy took me to be examined by a surgeon who specialized in women's nervous diseases. I think Daddy had to pay him extra to see me, and then I had to be escorted in through the back door. I didn't want to go, but I had no choice. The doctor was an old white man who told me he didn't often see wenches like me in his practice."

"Oh, Mary Ann," I said. Dread crept up my spine as a warning of how the story would unfold.

She was determined to tell us. "Dr. Diddley made me take off all my clothes, even my drawers and stockings. Then he told me to lie down on this hard bench he had, and spread my legs so he could study the evidence. I was so mortified I just about fell off when he held my breasts and squeezed each of my nipples until they stood up. Then he used his fingers to open up my coochie and find my clitoris. That was the problem, he said. He rubbed it one way, and then the other way, and he coaxed it to get big and asked if I was excited. I said no because I didn't know what he would do if I said yes.

"Dr. Diddley said, 'You mustn't lie to your doctor, my dear, because then I can't help you.' And he moved his finger in circles until I had a paroxysm—what he called it—and I wet the examining bench. Then he said, 'Hmm,' like that."

"He was most likely a swindler," I stormed, "not a real doctor at all."

"Well, a lot of folks thought he could cure whatever ailed a person," she replied. "If getting excited was a sign of nervous disease, that doctor had it bad. He did all kinds of things to me, and I couldn't stop him because I didn't want to find out what the diagnosis would be if I didn't co-operate. After he was finished, he said he had to consult with my father, and

I was afraid he would recommend putting me in the insane asylum."

"Did he?" I asked. Mary Ann's tale was turning my blood cold.

"No," she answered. "I guess he thought nothing could change my animal nature. Later, my father told me the doctor said he would operate on any white woman who showed such extreme signs of nervous excitability as I did, but in my case, he thought it best to let nature take its course. Daddy told me the doctor said I needed to be married right away. I don't think 'married' is the exact word he used."

"Men are idiots," I said, "except the Green Men. That includes you, Alfred." Alfred smiled.

"I could put up with anything," said Mary Ann, "as long as I could be with Charley." Anger and hopelessness competed in her expression. "But Miz Rosamund and my father agreed to send Charley away because of our bad influence on each other. Miz Rosamund said she wrote to her friends up North about it. Daddy told me Charley would have to pack her things and take the train to Philadelphia. I thought I would die without her."

Mary Ann took a deep breath of the close air in the cabin. "Are you both sure you want to hear the rest of my story? The last part isn't what you'd call uplifting."

"Oh yes. Your teacher was right, Mary Ann," I answered. "You are very good at dramatic presentations. Please continue." Alfred nodded in agreement.

"I wasn't allowed to leave the house at all, so the day before Charley was supposed to board the train, I packed a trunk and told Sam to deliver it to Charley for Miz Forrester. I said it was rags for quilts. That night, I snuck over to Miz Forrester's house and threw stones up at Charley's window until she saw me and came to the door to let me in.

"She was sure glad to see me! She had cut off her long brown hair, so it stood up all over her head. She made a comical sight, though I knew Miz Rosamund would pitch a fit. Charley brought me up the stairs to her own bed, and helped me out of my clothes in the dark because we didn't dare light any lamps. Everybody in those parts knew Miz Forrester always retired early.

"Charley was kissing her way down my neck to my bubbies, and I was just getting used to her head of hair like a field of mown hay when somebody pounded on the door as if the boogie man was chasing them.

"I ran to the window to look. I thought I would faint when I saw who all was out there. Papa was standing in front, as if he expected the door to open at any minute, and Miz Rosamund was there, and all our house servants—Sam, Rufus the Overseer, Sophy and Cook, as we called her.

"For a moment, I hoped I wouldn't have to go home, but then I realized how simple-minded I was. They weren't paying a social call. I whispered to Charley just to pretend we weren't there, but we both knew it was no use.

"Miz Forrester woke up and called out to ask who was there. I put my clothes back on as well as I could, but there was nothing I could do about my hair in the time we had. When Charley and I went to open the door, Miz Forrester was already speaking to my father. She was wearing a shawl over her nightgown, with one gray braid hanging down her back, and I prob'ly didn't look any more fit for company. As soon as my father saw me, he grabbed me by the shoulders and just pulled me along the way he would pull a mule. Miz Rosamund didn't have the strength to pull Charley like that, but she told her she was taking her home where she could keep an eye on her.

"They pushed us into the wagon they came in and brought us back to Cornford. I said I needed my trunk and Charley needed her things too, but Miz Rosamund said everything could be sent for. On the way, she told my father she thought we should both be horsewhipped, and she sounded serious as a judge. Daddy said he thought the perpetrator should learn the error of her ways, but he was a gentleman, so he would leave it to Providence.

"As soon as we all arrived at the big house, Miz Rosamund took Charley away while Daddy said he needed to speak to me about an urgent matter, and Sam had to come too because he was involved in it. We all went into the library where Daddy gave me a speech about how disappointed he was that I was turning my back on my fine education and all the other advantages he had given me. He said he was willing to let me get married right away because that was the best course.

"Then Sam asked me to marry him! He and Daddy had it all cooked up before they ever said a word to me. Daddy said he already gave Sam his freedom and he would write us both into his will as heirs to his estate.

"I knew very well that a lady is never supposed to raise her voice, but I yelled loud enough to wake my poor departed mama. 'What makes y'all think I want to get married?' I asked them. 'There's one person I love best in the world, and it's not Sam.' I begged his pardon for saying so, and said I hoped he understood my meaning. Sam said he understood me just fine because he knew a lady never says yes the first time. He was smiling as if he had heard something funny, and that was when I knew how useless it is for a woman to speak her mind to a man. My father said he hoped I would have a change of heart, but he wouldn't force me into it. He said he hoped I would settle down once Charley was gone. I asked for permission to see her off on the train, and Daddy said he wasn't sure that was a good idea, but he wouldn't oppose it because he couldn't help being an indulgent father, and he thought we needed to say our goodbyes properly.

"You can bet I didn't get a wink of sleep that night, and in the morning, I had to put on an old morning-gown that had faded from the sun because my favorite clothes were in my trunk at Miz Forrester's house. I looked a fright, and Charley didn't look her best either. Miz Rosamund made her wear a bonnet to cover her short hair.

"When we got to the train station, I still hoped there was a way for me to sneak on at the last minute, and go away with Charley before anyone could stop me. I didn't see how I could bear the disappointment if I had to stand on the platform, watching the train wheels turning faster and faster as they carried Charley away to a new life without me. I wanted to shake off the dust of the stupid old South.

"Charley wouldn't look at me in the station, and I thought it was because she didn't want to show her feelings in front of Papa and Miz Rosamund. Then some fancy woman in a gown with a scarlet bodice and black lace trimming, with a bonnet and parasol to match, came strutting right up to our little family group. 'Miz Charlotte,' she said as bold as you please, 'I'm so sorry to see you go.' She walked right up to Charley and kissed her on the cheek, and that was when I knew they were more than acquaintances. If you've ever met a lady of the evening, you know how they can give the most intimate messages without saying a word.

"'Excuse me,' I told her, 'I don't believe we've been introduced.'

"The hussy stared at me as if she had never heard such impertinence. 'Miz Mary Ann,' said Charley, 'this is Miz Lily Montmorency.' I didn't believe for a moment that was her real name, and I couldn't force myself to say I was pleased to meet her.

"'Miz Charlotte,' I said, 'I didn't know you had such an interesting friend.'

"Charley winked at me and said, 'You know I like the ladies.'

"Daddy cleared his throat. 'The train is due to arrive any minute, miss,' he told Charley, deliberately ignoring the one called Lily. Huh. She looked more like a poisonous plant. Daddy said, 'Your Aunt would like to give you her last instructions.'

"'I declare,' said the strumpet to Charley, looking sideways at me, 'Miz Charlotte, you may not care how anyone speaks to you, but I do. I'm sure your free-and-easy ways will suit you just fine up North. *Bon voyage, ma cherie.'*

"The train arrived with as much commotion as Charley's hussy made when she walked away from us, brushing every passer-by with her cowcatcher of a skirt. Miz Rosamund told Charley a lot of things I couldn't hear because of the roaring in my ears, and it wasn't all caused by the train or the crowd of people that were there to meet it.

"Charley boarded the train, and then she was waving at us through a window, just as I had imagined. Now I knew she would forget me as soon as the next gal came along, and I could hardly bear it. How quickly a dream can be destroyed forever! I didn't know if I would ever go up North, but I knew if I did it wouldn't be on account of her."

"Mary Ann," I exclaimed, "I wish I had been there to comfort you!" I wrapped her in my arms, and she held me tightly until she could speak again.

"Ohh," she sighed, "the worst of it was yet to come. War broke out, and then there was no train travel for anyone but soldiers. My father kept urging me to marry Sam because the future was uncertain and he wanted me to have a husband and a secure inheritance. I could see that Miz Rosamund didn't like that very much. She said if I didn't want to marry, I should find work so I wouldn't be such a burden on my family. She sure enough didn't mind having room and board at Cornford!

"Just when I thought things couldn't get any worse, my father had a seizure. When the doctor came, he said it was apoplexy, and all we could do was pray for him to pull through. When I went to see Daddy in the morning, I knew right away he was gone. His spirit had left his body.

"So then I had nobody on my side except Sam and the other house staff, and they had no power to stop Miz Rosamund from doing whatever she liked. In a few days, the house filled up with white folks I didn't even know, and she said they were all her family and friends. When she invited me to meet

Mr. Gregory Towne, the captain of the *Dixieland*, I thought
she was looking to marry me off with a dowry to get me out
of her way. Marriage would have been a sight better than
what they had planned!

"Captain Towne offered one hundred dollars for me, and
Miz Rosamund said that was acceptable. I told them both
there was a slight problem with their business transaction
because I was a free woman of color, and I didn't agree to
be sold. I said if they didn't believe I was Master Cornford's
daughter and heiress, they could read his papers and the en-
rollment list at Miz Brightman's school. Miz Rosamund told
him I was an impudent, lying wench that would settle down
once I knew who was in charge, so the captain should use
whatever measures were necessary.

"When I saw he had shackles and a pistol with him, I tried
to escape, but I couldn't get away. No matter how much I
fought and screamed, no one could help me, so I was taken
to the ship with just the belongings I could gather up with
the captain watching, including my underthings.

"The captain didn't want me for his own use, so I think he
intended to sell me along with his cargo. In the meanwhile,
though, he didn't care what his First Mate did to me. He was
a dirty, drunken rat of a man who thought I was brought
along to satisfy him on the voyage. By then, I decided I would
rather die than be his concubine, so when I had the chance
to steal a knife, I used it. And that's how you found me."

"Blimey," remarked Alfred. "Good riddance to bad rubbish.
Well done, love!" I applauded, and Alfred joined in.

Mary Ann looked pleased. "Emily must tell hers next," she
proposed.

"I'll take the last turn," added Alfred. "I don't mind." The
truth was that neither of us wanted to tell our life-stories
immediately after hearing Mary Ann's. By general consensus,
we postponed the following tales to another day.

Twelve

Fortune and Men's Eyes

AFTER THE STORM, THE SKY WAS BRIGHT
and the ocean glassy. All the Green Men spent as much time
on deck as possible, vying with playful breezes to create fan-
ciful shapes in the smoke from their homemade cigars.

Roger and Martin looked weary but determined when
they addressed the assembled crew. "The storm blew us off-
course," Roger explained, "and it shall probably cost us several days of lost time. We're on-course for the Bahamas now,
and a good wind may give us an advantage. We're all alive
and well enough to work. We have nothing to fear, men." I
looked steadily at my husband. "And ladies," he added.

I could find no fault in Roger's intentions, and blaming the
storm that toyed with our lives would be fruitless. There was
nothing for us all to do but cling to hope.

MARY ANN, ALFRED AND I RESUMED OUR
exchange of life-histories as we stood at the rail, studying
the ocean's ever-changing moods. "I was born in Jamaica to
English parents," I began. By the time I explained why they
arranged to send us, their children, to England for our safety,
several of the Green Men were more attentive than an audience in a London theater on opening night.

I tried to sum up my affair with Lucy in seemly language,
omitting all mention of the candle under the bed-clothes, _99_

but I was met by a chorus of chuckles and "Oh, what tricks" and "Then what did she do?" Hopwell, who appeared fully recovered from the wound Alfred had given him, shouted merrily, "Headmistress ought to have given you both good whippings!" He licked his lips. I couldn't be sure whether he spoke in jest.

Martin bustled closer to the circle that had gathered round me. "Hopwell!" he remonstrated. "Ladies don't need to be disciplined like men. They are made of finer stuff." He struggled to express himself more clearly. "I mean to say, the ladies in our midst have earned our respect. They have every right to love in their own way without being verbally assaulted."

"Bonnyshanks," Jackson suggested, "Bend over one of the smashers so Captain can apply the cat to your bouncy pink bum. When the ladies see that, they might get a taste for it." Martin turned redder than I had yet seen him, but I now knew him well enough to suspect that he relished his embarrassment. And all the other Green Men relished it too.

Jackson's comment and the general response gave me pause for thought. I put my mending aside and addressed all those on deck. "Friends, comrades in arms, we are waiting to see what fate has in store for us. Perhaps we shall all outwit the law and live to tell our tale for many years to come, or perhaps we shall never again set foot on dry land. We all cast our lots in together when we boarded this ship on our quest for pleasure, love and beauty. Are we not united against every authority which forbids those things?

"Aye!" responded a chorus of lusty male voices.

I attempted a bearing like that of Joan of Arc addressing the French troops. "Here is what I propose," I told my shipmates. "Mary Ann, Alfred and I agreed to tell each other our histories whilst we were confined during the storm. Let everyone here take a turn doing the same, and freely reveal all we have done to harm others, and what others have done to harm us. We can imagine that this is Judgment Day. At the end of each tale, there shall be a general vote to decide whether the tale-teller deserves to give or receive a flogging. Women are included, and the majority rules."

"Confessions! Judgments! Floggings! We can give 'em and we can take 'em!" shouted several of the men, smacking each other's shoulders, chests and backsides.

Roger pushed his way toward me. "See here, Emily," he objected. "I'm the captain of the *Black Swan*, and I make the rules on this ship. Of course, I always consider what is best for my—everyone in my charge. I will allow a general vote, but I alone will decide the final outcome. Does anyone here raise an objection to that?"

"No, Captain!" responded several of the men. The rest were silent, but no one appeared to be mutinous.

"Captain," Mary Ann remarked primly, "Miz Emily hasn't finished her story."

"True enough, Miss Cornford," he replied, "But I believe I know her history better than anyone else here, and I may discipline anyone who judges her unfairly."

A visible frisson of delight ran through all those on deck as they contemplated the possibilities. I could hardly have devised a better plan for raising the general esprit de corps.

"I haven't much left to tell," I resumed. "Lucy came out into Society and cut me dead on orders from her parents."

"My parents as well," Roger interjected, "Sir Frederick and Lady Caroline Tingley-Jones. As their eldest son and heir, I am a greater disappointment to them than my sister Lucy. She, it seems, could be reformed enough to present them with grandchildren."

So could we, I thought, and if our lovers wouldn't object, Roger could still satisfy his parents' dynastic ambitions. I resolved to discuss this with him at a better time.

"I met the Captain and the First Mate," I continued, "when they—um, invited me to dine with them. Your captain proposed marriage and I accepted him. We were to cross the ocean and fight slavery in the American war. That's what I told my parents in the letter I left for them when I slipt away in the night. The rest you know."

"On board," Roger smoothly explained, "you accepted Martin as your other bridegroom on our wedding night, then you discovered the only other female on the ship. You protected her from the consequences of her disguise and became her intimate friend. After we informed you of our true mission, you traded your useful needle for a sword, and proved yourself as ruthless as any man of us. You recognized a kindred spirit when you found Miss Cornford covered in the blood of the man she had just killed, and you refused to be parted from her."

Did Roger wish to flog us both?

Mary Ann and I both began to speak at once. Roger raised his hands for silence. "In short," he concluded, "Emily, you are a perfectly darling wife. I could not have found a woman better suited to my taste."

"Hurray for Missus Captain!" shouted a chorus of voices.

Subsequently, fifteen of the crew voted to have me flogged. Twenty voted for my acquittal, and ten (including Mary Ann) voted to give me permission to flog Roger for his unchivalrous description of me. Twelve voted to let me flog Martin for practice, and seven voted to let me flog Mary Ann for not knowing her place. Roger observed that several men had voted more than once, and he closed the discussion by threatening to flog anyone who continued to speak.

Roger declared me safe from any participation in flogging except by my choice. I declined for the moment, still feeling perplexed about the significance of flogging as punishment, reward or diversion.

Alfred began his (or her) life-story: "Me mum and dad had four sons and three daughters before me, so when I came along, I wasn't much noticed. I never felt like a girl, no matter how much anyone tried to beat it into me. When me older brother went away to sea, I wanted to go too. I went to the dock to look at the ships whenever I could. I smuggled meself aboard, and when I heard one of the other sailors talking about a group of degenerates called the Green Men's Society, it gave me hope, if you see what I mean. Captain Roger took me in, and I'll never forget it."

Alfred's story seemed to make up in pathos what it lacked in length. "Have you ever been in love, Alfred?" I asked slyly.

"Alfred?" demanded one of the men. "That's Sweeper!"

"It wouldn't trouble you much to call him by the name he chose for himself!" I retorted. "I thought fellowship was the rule on this good ship."

"The fellowship of fellows," replied the malcontent. "One woman on a ship is bad luck enough, but there's three of you here, includin' a nigger that thinks she's a bloody princess. No wonder we were blown off-course!"

"Sweeper needs a good flogging!" shouted another man. I suspected that he was more offended by a misleading appearance of manhood than by trousers per se.

Roger seemed likely to order floggings all round until Mary Ann caught his sleeve and said something in his ear.

"Attend to Miss Cornford!" he commanded everyone on board.

"Gentlemen," she addressed them in a coquettish tone. "I believe the one you call Sweeper requires discipline, and I feel most entitled to apply it. I can't explain the injury he did to me, but I assure you it is entirely unspeakable. There has been a moral breach that demands correction."

Muttering followed as the men tried to puzzle out the reason for Mary Ann's interest in Alfred's backside. Despite the general confusion, forty voted for flogging. No one could deny that the "ayes" formed a majority.

"Sir," pleaded the pale bosun, "may I keep my trousers on, for the love of God?"

"You may," answered Roger, "but they shall be scant protection. Miss Cornford, I recommend the cane." Martin disappeared and soon returned bearing the instrument.

Two men led Alfred to one of the smashers, bent him over it and held him in place.

Mary Ann accepted the cane and handled it lovingly, then swished it through the air in a practice strike. "Prepare yourself, Alfred," she warned. "You look too invitin'."

She raised the cane and brought it down upon the seat of Alfred's trousers, which were pulled tight by his position. Alfred flinched, but made no sound.

"That's the way, girl!" shouted an eager witness. The man standing behind him pressed rhythmically against his buttocks whilst reaching into the trousers of the man in front to fondle his cock.

I looked about me, and saw a bulge in every pair of trousers except Mary Ann's. Despite the prickling of my conscience, I felt a parallel prickling in my own.

"Six strokes," instructed Roger, "and no more, Miss, or each one in excess shall be repaid to your own derrière."

She paused dramatically after each stroke, and delivered the next with increased vigor. By the fifth, Alfred was moaning, and so was his audience. Mary Ann swung her arm cleanly on the sixth stroke. Alfred responded with a violent jerk and an uncouth shout.

When the bosun was raised upright, his face was wet, yet his expression was peaceful. Something about Alfred's status seemed to have changed, and I no longer sensed hostility in the air. Mary Ann dropt the cane upon the deck, and threw her arms round her victim. "We're even now," she told him. "Honey, I didn't want to stop."

Martin retrieved the cane and wiped it with his handkerchief. Roger wrapt a protective arm round his plump shoulders.

Men all over the deck were rubbing their own and each other's naked cocks, trying to co-ordinate their movements. Groins were pressed against receptive bottoms. Hair on chests and thighs moved in the breeze as clothing lay ignored under bodies that glowed with sweat.

A thin sailor with a lined face and gray hair approached Alfred as soon as Mary Ann released him. "Lad," said the old man, "I've an ointment that would help your bum heal. If you come with me, I'll give you the relief you need." Despite the weight of his years, the venerable sailor wore the cunning look of the young sea rat he must have been in the time of Napolean. We all knew what sort of relief he was offering.

"Thank you, sir," replied Alfred, and genuine gratitude shone in his eyes. The smart of a caning was probably a mere bee-sting compared to the constant pain of his one-sided love for his idol and (much as I hated to consider it) that of my own defection. I hoped that Alfred would always find consolation in some form.

"Ladies," crooned Roger with a smile, "that was a stirring performance. May I call you Mary Ann?"

"Surely," she replied. "We're no strangers to each other, Captain."

"Indeed," he replied, "but I wish to deepen our acquaintance, dear. As you expressed it, every moral imbalance needs to be set right. If we four are to be companions for as long as our lives last, we have no need of reticence amongst us. Emily, as my wife, you freely gave yourself to me and my beloved Martin. Mary Ann, will you give me the same liberty for Emily's sake? You've made my rod as hard as iron."

"Yes, for my sake, Mary Ann," I smiled, almost laughing. "Please borrow my husband. I don't mind if you don't." On impulse, I asked for help from the ever-reliable Martin. "I think we four ought to indulge ourselves right here, in the fresh air. We'll form a compelling tableau for anyone who might be watching."

"Miz Emily," laughed Mary Ann. "You are full of interesting suggestions. Captain, my coochie would like to get a taste of you as well, but I hope you don't plan to fill my belly."

"I assure you, Mary Ann," he responded, "I have no desire to become a father in present circumstances. I shall waste my seed like the sinner that I am."

Without further ado, Roger seized Mary Ann in his arms and they kissed with equal passion. He soon shed his trousers, revealing a very hard cock; the sight reminded me of why my wedding-night deflowering was so uncomfortable. I had come so far since then that I wondered if I could now accommodate him more easily.

Martin and I pulled the sleeves of Mary Ann's shirt off her arms and raised the garment over her head. Roger removed her trousers by helping her to lift her feet out of them, one at a time, as he gripped each of her thighs to steady her.

Mary Ann always seemed to gain grace and presence when deprived of clothing. In the present instance, she glowed like a gilded Venus.

I felt the sudden sting of jealousy. Was I really willing to let Roger claim my Mary Ann (or Ekineba, a name he didn't know) as part of his "harem"? As I watched her fold her clothing and lay it on the deck (treating us all to a fine view of her buttocks), then spread herself on her back, I knew it was too late for me to prevent what was about to happen.

Roger lowered himself atop her. He rested his weight on his elbows as he suckled one of her nipples. Mary Ann winked at me as if to remind me that what she was doing with Roger was a lark, the scratching of a mutual itch, but not an expression of love on either side.

I remembered that not one of us was guaranteed to return to Civilization, as it is called, and if we did, our safety was hardly assured. The only comfort we had was the pleasure of the moment, and who was I to begrudge it to anyone?

As if reading my thoughts, Martin pulled me to him and kissed me. His moist bare skin pressed against my shirt, and I felt ridiculously overdressed. Although I couldn't pull my attention away from the sight of Roger's square, muscular bottom pumping with increasing vigor as Mary Ann met him thrust for thrust, Martin managed to undress me. As soon as my trousers were off, he slid two searching fingers into my very wet cunt.

Poor Martin. I realized that he had proven himself as able an English sailor as any man on board, yet even the Green Men didn't give him the respect which was his due. "Dear Martin," I whispered so that no one else could hear, "I hope we'll always be friends."

"Emily," he replied, digging in his fingers in a most delicious way, "you are my favorite girl." He gently withdrew from me just as my excitement was rising. "Come sit in my lap."

Martin seated himself on the deck, then helped me to lower myself onto his upstanding red cock so that we could embrace at the same time. I was able to bounce up and down as I chose, ensuring that he stroked all the right spots inside me. Within moments, however, he lifted me with a warning grunt, and I stood up just in time to see his cock erupt like a fountain.

I heard Roger playfully chiding Mary Ann: "See what effect you have on me, woman." I glanced over to see his own cock in a similar state.

Our two men looked pleased, but I could see that Mary Ann was no more satisfied than I was. "Ladies," said Roger. He smiled at Mary Ann, then at me, and more meaningfully at Martin.

"Gentlemen," I answered. We four had reached such an understanding that further words were unnecessary.

"Very stimulating," remarked Mary Ann. "Emily honey, shall we leave our husbands to their own devices?" A round of laughter answered her question, and we exchanged partners.

Mary Ann spread her thighs apart, and I buried my tongue in her sweet center as though it were the most delicious pudding on earth. She soon writhed and moaned in a way I recognized, and I reached into her to coax out every last wriggle and sigh.

After taking a moment to recompose herself, Mary Ann showed a desire to outdo me in lovemaking. She pressed her face into my neck and urged me on with her wordless language. Three of her fingers plumbed my depths, and then I felt a refreshing wind on my exposed limbs.

"Wind, lads!" shouted a man from further aft. Raising my head slightly, I could see that several of the Green Men had returned to the rigging. Their devotion to duty in the midst of an orgy made a great impression on me.

"Wind!" came the echoing shout from men in various states of undress and distraction. I looked up to see all our sails billowing like enormous petticoats, filled to bursting with the power to bring us to land. Mary Ann brought her other hand smartly down upon one of my arse-cheeks. I spent deliriously.

Thirteen

Winged Progress

LIKE THE BREATH OF ANGELS, THE WIND never failed us. Day after day, the *Black Swan* cut a frothy white path through the waves.

ONE AFTERNOON, FINDING MARTIN UNCHAR-acteristically idle as he gazed over the rails, I approached him on the subject of his bouncy pink bum, as his shipmate had described it. "Martin," I said quietly, not wanting to startle him out of his reverie, "please pardon my curiosity, but do you enjoy being flogged?"

He gazed at me and then at the ocean as though it could provide him with eloquence. "Aye," he said at last. "If you're seeking a simple answer, Emily, that would be it." He paused. "Perhaps 'enjoy' is not the most accurate description. A good flogging cleanses the soul. It connects the one who gives it to the one who receives it. It communicates more honestly than words." He looked into my eyes. "What happens to men's arses also happens to their cocks, darling, if you'll excuse the crudeness of my explanation. I suppose it's different for ladies."

"Not so much," I mused. "Alfred was born female, and I'm sure sh-he experienced what you've described, in some measure at least. If it were only a matter of biology, I suppose most women would offer their backsides at every opportunity. But

Martin, you can't imagine how much I dread being struck as a punishment for disobedience. When I was in school, we all feared the cane. Girls who were caned were never exactly the same afterwards. As far as I could see, it didn't make them more conscientious. It killed some vital spark in them."

Martin swept me into his arms and pressed me to his chest. "Ah. So did flogging in the Queen's Navy, me girl, and that was the purpose of it. We're all here because of that, just as much as we wish to keep our necks free from the noose. The laws of England were never meant to benefit all men equally, whatever anyone says about the Magna Carta."

"The laws don't benefit women at all," I added, "even in America, no matter what anyone says, and the North seems no better than the South. Martin, if we ever set foot in England again, I am going to join a group of disreputable harridans who march down the streets with banners in support of women's legal rights. I shall expect you to defend me against all criticism, and help me to escape from jail if necessary."

"So I will, Emily," he chuckled, "but then your husband might teach your saucy bottom a lesson about putting yourself in harm's way."

"I could do that for him," laughed Mary Ann from behind me. She squeezed both my arse-cheeks through my trousers, making me jump.

"I should think not!" I protested. "You, of all women on earth, ought to lead the parade."

"For the Rights of Woman," Martin explained. "Mary Ann, I presume you need no introduction to this fiery subject." She rolled her eyes at me in a way that spoke more clearly than words. "Or," Martin continued, "to the efficacy of the cat, the cane, the paddle, and sundry other clever implements. Not least of which is the human hand." He flourished his own right hand for our admiration.

I had not imagined Martin smacking any part of anyone else's body. The possibilities suggested by his capable hand were strangely exciting.

"Martin honey," flirted Mary Ann, "we are in complete agreement."

"Emily needs further persuasion," he laughed.

"Surely the spirit of the thing makes all the difference," I told them both. "No one in the modern world deserves to be beaten into saying what they don't mean."

Roger joined our party. "Emily, you are a very Portia," he proclaimed. He encircled my waist and kissed me on the cheek. "You were born to defend the victims of persecution in a court of law."

"Yet Nature herself is democratic," Martin explained. Warming to his subject, he added: "Everyone has an arse, a bottom, a bum, or a derrière, and the abundance of words to describe this part of our bodies speaks to its own abundance. Why do we each have two mounds of flesh that stick out behind us, if not to attract the attention of everyone who follows? And these impudent cheeks are designed to be struck repeatedly without any lasting damage. Bottoms bounce back."

"And if you part them," Roger added, "you find a most delightful entrance to the Cave of the Mysteries." The prickling that I felt whilst watching Alfred's ordeal returned to my quim and spread to my tighter entrance.

As Roger spoke, he pressed the front of his trousers against the seat of Martin's. The two men began a sort of backwards-and-forwards waltz.

Mary Ann imitated their movements by thrusting her hips into the air. I thought of her own bottom, and wondered how she would look tied naked to a whipping-post, awaiting the lash.

Oh, what a brute I was in secret! How could I denounce the evils of slavery without being the rankest hypocrite?

As if in response to my thought, she imitated Roger by pressing herself against me. "Emily," she remarked sweetly. "I need to practice my aim." She chuckled, making her meaning perfectly clear. "We're women, but we're both in a queer sort of navy, and we need to be ready for anything that happens."

I couldn't help remembering the thrill of watching Lucy draw back her bow to let an arrow fly to the heart of its target, or the thrill of taking my turn. Whilst watching Mary Ann apply the cane, I had secretly wished to take her place, but at this moment, the heat of her belly and loins awakened my bottom to the pleasures of surrender.

"You are very wise, dear heart," I told her. "Let's practice in our cabin." Alfred seemed to be permanently installed in another part of the ship. "By turns," I added. "If I can't bear to sit after you've practiced on me, you must be prepared to wear the same stripes. And your bottom is a bigger target than mine."

"My hands are bigger than yours too," she reminded me, "but what's fair is fair. My whole body belongs to you, Miz Captain." And so we adjourned to private quarters to learn how much we could each give and receive, knowing that our two husbands, although vastly more experienced in such matters, were still exploring their own and each other's mysteries.

TIME PASSED MORE QUICKLY THAN BEFORE. When New Providence appeared on the horizon, most of us gathered together at the rail, whooping and leaning into the spray as though our collective will could speed us forward. The island shone as green as an emerald and as seductive as a mirage.

Coming to port felt like a dream. I held Mary Ann's hand whilst Roger and Martin were busy dropping anchor and other men handled the sails. Someone diligently hoisted the Union Jack, as though it were a talisman which could protect us from suspicion.

How would we women present ourselves to the townspeople of Nassau?

"Ladies," said Martin, moving his shoulders uneasily, "Roger and I must search out opportunities for trade."

"We understand, Martin," I replied, trying not to sound bitter. "Mary Ann and I would attract too much attention."

And so, like shackled women in more primitive times, we remained out of sight as we waited for news. How I wished we could have waited in a comfortable inn, soaking in a tub of warm, fresh water!

Our impatience grew as the hours passed.

NIGHT HAD FALLEN WHEN UNKNOWN VOICES and bobbing lanterns alerted us to the return of our husbands, accompanied by new (and useful, I hoped) acquaintances. "Mr. Greenleaf and Mr. Featherlight!" gushed the tenor voice of someone whose boots clattered up the gangplank, seeming to follow Roger's more measured tread. "Sirs, we are most honored."

"Honored," repeated a man with a deeper voice, "to accept your hospitality, but of course, we only do business by daylight."

"Sirs," said the first man, who sounded out of breath. "We are most interested in your bales. Of course, the quality of cotton depends on the conditions in which it was grown. You haven't told us the grade of your harvest."

Mary Ann and I were sequestered in the captain's cabin, where we had helped each other to dress for guests or for our first promenade on dry land. She had taught me to help do her hair up in little plaits all over her head, and she helped me to dress mine the same way. Due to our shortage of washing water, my hair was hardly more slippery than hers. Our plaits held firm without any ribbons or hairpins.

"Emily, darling! Mary Ann!" Roger summoned us to a meeting with his new business associates.

We gathered in our makeshift mess-hall, which contained a table and a set of chairs. Roger and Martin ushered in two men whom they introduced to us as Mr. Jeremiah Banks and his nephew, Mr. Bartholomew Banks, of the West Indies Trading Company.

The uncle (the taller man, with gray jowls and whiskers) and the boyish nephew looked startled to see us both, and their gazes kept returning to our hair. I felt increasingly out of sorts, and I hoped these tradesmen would prove different from the officers of the Union Navy. Mary Ann clearly resented being introduced as my "companion," by which Martin implied that she was a sort of lady's-maid. But she was my companion!

"Mrs. Greenleaf," said Mr. Bargain Senior, "you must be very proud of your husband's valor in the war. And how touching a demonstration of your mutual opposition to slavery." He smiled patronizingly at Mary Ann.

I clutched her hand under my skirt, hoping to convey to her that attacking this man would not be in our general interests, financially or in any other sense.

"And I'm sure you are both very proud that your cause has triumphed at last," he announced.

If Roger, Martin and Mary Ann were as surprised as I was, none of them showed it. "We were blown off-course by a storm at sea," Roger explained, "which delayed our arrival here by several weeks. We have heard no news of world affairs, gentlemen."

Mr. Banks Junior almost jumped off his chair. "Then allow us to be the first to bring you good tidings!" he beamed. He reminded me of an eager puppy. "The United States has been reunited by the Union victory, and President Lincoln set all the slaves free before he was murdered by a deranged southern assassin. Democracy can't be stopped. A new era has begun."

"Perhaps trade will improve," added Mr. Banks Senior, "under more equitable conditions."

"With international peace," Mr. Banks Junior hoped aloud.

"We would be delighted if you would dine with us at the Prancing Pig," said the older man. "It is a reputable inn where they set a very good table. At our expense, of course, which can be deducted later."

"Once we've decided on the value of your cargo," added the nephew.

So it was settled that after the two Bankses had inspected the cotton and tobacco in our hold, Roger, Martin and I would join them for dinner.

There was the issue of Mary Ann. "May my companion join us?" I asked, choking on the simpering tone I felt forced to adopt. "She has been so stalwart through all our ordeals at sea, and if my husband is ultimately to pay for her meal, I can't see why there would be any difficulty."

Roger responded to this cue. "Yes, of course I would like Mary Ann to join us," he asserted. She held her fire and remained silent.

"Private room," the nephew muttered to his uncle, who seemed disconcerted by what he undoubtedly regarded as our English eccentricity in support of a moral crusade.

Mr. Banks Senior could not hold out against our united force, and so our merry little party followed him off the *Black Swan*.

If you have never tried to walk on solid earth whilst managing full skirts after living in trousers on a pitching, rolling ship for many weeks, you can hardly imagine how ungracefully Mary Ann and I stumbled along. It was all I could do not to fall against her and carry her with me to the ground.

THE PRANCING PIG WAS A DELIGHTFUL HAVEN of welcoming chairs, a blazing hearth, and linen-covered tables groaning with food and drink. Roger, Martin, Mary Ann and I politely declined to partake of seafood, despite the recommendations of the two Bankses. When my order of roast beef arrived, I felt as if I could spend just from its enticing scent. We ate until we were all in a delightfully good humor. All the men drank rum, and Mr. Banks Senior took the liberty of ordering tonic wine for the ladies.

In the midst of plenty, I was unwilling to seem ungracious, but I wondered how I could bear to continue playing the role of a lady in public for the rest of my life. Mary Ann's comical expressions, directed to me alone, served to remind me that all such social occasions were a kind of theater, not to be taken seriously.

At the end of the meal, I was abruptly cheated out of playing a role in the negotiations. The two Bankses, Junior and Senior, apologetically asked Mary Ann and me to remain in the private room, where we would be served tea, whilst the gentlemen would adjourn to an airier space to "talk business" over brandy and cigars. The Bankses said they would fetch us once they had reached agreement.

Having complied thus far, Mary Ann and I swallowed our outrage and accepted this arrangement.

Our attempts to find each other's most responsive parts through layers of fabric were rudely interrupted by a bellowing English voice. "Sir Roger Tingley-Jones!" resonated through an open doorway.

"No, I'm afraid you're—" Roger responded.

"Beg pardon, man, but if you're not the new Lord Lowerend, you must be a close relation."

Mary Ann and I rushed into the public dining-room to see a corpulent, bushy-whiskered, brass-buttoned officer of the Royal Navy commanding attention from everyone present. As far as I could see, Roger and Martin had no means of escape.

I considered distracting the general company by swooning or pretending to find a rat under my skirt, but Roger and Martin stood up to face the captain. My blood ran cold as I realized that they had decided to cease running like fugitive rats themselves.

"May I have—" Roger began.

"Captain Julius Hatchway of Her Majesty's Ship *Hercules*, at your service, Sir," answered the captain. "I have the honor of claiming Lady Tingley-Jones as an old and dear friend. Not that she's old at all," he added. "A terrible shame it was about her husband, such a sudden shock for her. And now the heir is missing. Her eldest son seems to have given up his life for the Northern States in that blasted American war."

The captain caught sight of me and Mary Ann. "I do beg your pardon, ladies," he purred, sounding like a lion trying to be charming. "My language is more suitable for sailors than for polite company." His eyes twinkled.

You know who Roger is, I thought, *and what we've done.*

"Do you mean Lady Caroline Tingley-Jones of Cornwall?" ventured Roger. "Wife of Frederick, mother of Roger, Wilbert, Lucy, Amelia, and Lionel?"

"The very same," boomed the captain, apparently wishing to inform all the inn's clientele. "But she's a widow since the baronet passed away in a dreadful hunting accident."

"Go for it, guv'nor," muttered Martin to Roger, not quietly enough.

"I am Roger Tingley-Jones," he announced. No one applauded, but I was sure I heard a muted gasp or two.

"Then what a fortunate coincidence that we've met here in Nassau!" responded the captain.

Nonsense, I thought. *You've been following us ever since the Black Swan arrived in the harbor, and possibly before then.*

"Is my mother—d-does she—?" stuttered Roger.

"She misses you terribly, man," replied the captain. "When the prodigal son returns, all will be forgiven, as it says in the Bible. I have her Ladyship's word on it." He lowered his voice by a decibel or two. "How could any mother refuse to welcome her son if he's a war hero? You know how our nation feels about slavery in the seething tropics of the southern states, young sir, and why it couldn't stand unchallenged in the modern world. You took it on yourself to fight for the right, and every English man, woman and child loves you for it."

"He wasn't alone," Martin pointed out.

Roger recovered. "Allow me to introduce my esteemed First Mate," he said to the captain, "Mr. Martin Bonnyshanks."

After an exchange of meaningless pleasantries, Roger introduced me as his wife, and then Mary Ann and the Messrs. Banks to the captain who had brought us such momentous news. Bustling waiters pushed two tables together so that we could all be seated together like a large, respectable family.

"In less exceptional circumstances," confided the captain in Roger's ear, loudly enough to be overheard, "stealing a ship from Her Majesty, even one which is waiting to be chopped into firewood, might not be forgiven, Sir Robin Hood, but our gracious Queen won't order a hero to be hanged. This dark lass you've rescued from a slave plantation could plead your case. You could sell tickets for a quid apiece—" The captain paused as Mary Ann fixed her burning gaze on his face—"to finance a charitable foundation for former slaves." He leaned closer to Roger. "You lucky rogue."

And so our business abroad was concluded in one evening: the Bankses offered enough for our cotton and tobacco to enable us to repair and outfit the *Black Swan* for her home voyage across the Atlantic, accompanied by the *Hercules*.

Home! This singing word echoed in my mind all through the following fortnight as we made our preparations.

And for four of us, that word applied specifically to Roger's ancient, wind-worn family seat, Tingley Towers.

Fourteen

A Queer State of Affairs

BEFORE WE COULD SET SAIL ON THE LAST leg of our voyage, a significant number of Green Men jumped ship. The siren song of dry land proved irresistible for them.

"Chartreuse stripes!" exclaimed Jackson, observing a passing lady as a group of us made our way through the town on an expedition for supplies. "I fancy a waistcoat of that material, Missus Emily."

"And what a perfect shade to set off a complexion like a rotten lime," responded Hopwell. "Now there's a pair of trousers." He turned his head to follow the owner of the snug trousers as he passed in the opposite direction.

"You're gawking at a pair of thighs, man," retorted Jackson. "And a few things between."

Amongst the townspeople of Nassau, I was in constant anxiety that the Green Men's indiscreet remarks would provoke hostility. However, the town seemed remarkably hospitable, or perhaps coarsened by its history as a port for all ships.

As soon as Roger and Martin had paid each man for his share of the sold booty, I was so besieged with orders for clothing that I could not possibly complete all the work in time, even with Mary Ann as my assistant. And, truth be told, she lacked the necessary patience and skill.

When Alfred asked me for a new suit of clothes, I couldn't refuse. Measuring his compact body (made hard and tight through the chest and back by a binding cloth), I touched him shamelessly, and found my way under the harness that held his leather sausage.

Without a word, Alfred spread his legs to give me access to his hidden grotto and the little nubbin that he would never acknowledge in words.

I teased this powerful knot of flesh until it swelled, and its owner sighed and quivered. "Alfred," I whispered. "It's ever so big."

His climax wet my fingers and gave me a sweet memory to cherish after our last farewells. I knew that Alfred had no intention of returning to England.

As quickly as possible, I outfitted Alfred with a new shirt, jacket and trousers, all of fine cotton, and they seemed to have the magical power to transform him into a strutting dandy.

Dear Reader, you may choose to believe that the ability to change one's form is impossible in our scientific age. If so, I shall leave your belief undisturbed. Suffice it to say that after Mary Ann brought Alfred with her to find a practitioner of gris-gris or voodoo, Alfred's voice was deeper and his jaw squarer than before. And when we three gathered for an evening of serious pleasure in the room I shared with Mary Ann in the Prancing Pig, we women had cause to believe that a process had begun which would continue until Alfred's body matched his spirit.

Whether Alfred's heart would recover when his idol was far from him was a matter for speculation and hope. As I knew by the time I kissed Alfred goodbye, hearts change. Perhaps that is their greatest strength.

AT LAST, OUR ANCHOR WAS RAISED AND OUR sails unfurled by a crew which had diminished by sixteen men. The deserters bade us farewell and we wished them happiness in their new home, where they have undoubtedly raised the general standards of taste.

The wind favored us, and we sailed into the wide ocean. In the following weeks, Mary Ann and I had to stand watch at the tiller by turns, having learned from Roger and Martin. All hands were needed to guide the *Black Swan* back to England.

If you read the newspapers, you probably know that we were greeted by a marching band when we disembarked at Penzance, and Admiral Bilge resigned from the Royal Navy that very week in protest against the shocking lapse in public morality.

Sadly, the *Black Swan* herself had no future as a working ship. She was reclaimed by the government to be turned into a museum of slavery. In due course, she was populated by wax figures dressed in rags and joined at the ankles by chains. Our old ship proved as popular as Madame Tussaud's, but Mary Ann refused to mingle with the crowds that gathered on board to hear tour guides explain the horrors of whippings and forced labor.

MANY QUEER THINGS HAPPENED AS A DIRECT consequence of our return from our adventures, but my treatment by some representatives of Society was exactly what I expected. Upon our arrival, the widowed Lady Caroline Tingley-Jones appeared as a sombre figure in black to meet her son and his hangers-on. She seemed particularly surprised to see Mary Ann, but Martin and I did not escape her perplexed scrutiny.

"Welcome back to England, Roger," she told him, and her tone expressed a lifetime of dashed hopes. "I've brought the clarence." Apparently as an afterthought, she added, "Late congratulations on joining our family, Emily, even though Sir Frederick and I were not consulted."

"There was no time, Mother," snapped Roger, "and the present time could be better spent than in wishing the past were otherwise." He explained further that, in the present, Martin and Mary Ann would accompany us to Tingley Towers, where they would take up permanent residence.

AND SO WE ALL BUNDLED OURSELVES AND our belonging into a carriage designed for four passengers, where we were as cozy as a litter of puppies in a basket. The press of flesh and the bouncing ride over cobblestones produced a predictable reaction in the men, as I saw from the condition of their trousers, seated as I was on Mary Ann's lap. From time to time, she reached up discreetly to tickle my bubbies. We all grew impatient to reach our destination and settle ourselves in our separate living quarters.

Studying Lady Caroline's stiffly-corseted bodice and unhappy expression, I formed a plan. For her emergence into half-mourning six months after the death of her husband, I would make her a gown of dark mauve cotton which would please her in spite of herself. Pleasure and beauty would triumph over rank and prejudice.

No sooner did we arrive at Tingley Towers than we sought out the most comfortable, modern wing, and claimed our quarters. Neither Lady Caroline nor her other children needed to know that Martin slept in Roger's bed much more often than I did, or that Mary Ann's modest room served as storage space. The servants didn't acknowledge that anything was out of the ordinary, but guests sometimes remarked on their curious air of simmering mirth.

Several days after our arrival, I sent word to the local inn, where I found several of the Green Men. As I hoped, Dujour was amongst them, and thus I acquired a chief assistant and several apprentices for my dressmaking business. Eventually, my designs were much sought-after, and I had more trade than I could accommodate until I had found more apprentices amongst professional actors and the swans who adored dressing in "drag." My Green Men made frequent trips to London, where they recruited employees for me as diligently as anyone had ever recruited young men into the Navy.

Lady Caroline simply couldn't keep vulgar trade off the ancestral premises of Lord and Lady Lowerend, as Roger and I came to be known. Her marriage to Captain Hatchway after two years of widowhood seemed to be her way of separating herself from our household.

HOWEVER, LET ME RETURN TO THE BEGINning of my life in Cornwall. The queer place we four came to occupy in Society was as distinctive in its way as the rocky coast and the ancient Cornish language. Dear Reader, you can best understand our position if I explain events in their logical order.

Roger and I, with the Widow Tingley-Jones, were invited to the Palace to receive the Queen's thanks for cementing an alliance between the British Empire and the growing economic empire of the United States. As the story of our heroic mission became public knowledge, Mary Ann became an object of general obsession.

An eager young man with ink-stained fingers traveled from London to Tingley Towers and would not be refused an interview with our rescued slave. Katie, our newest maid, announced Mr. Elijah Scribbler. Without giving the matter sufficient thought, I brought him to the parlor to meet Mary Ann. What followed was like a scene from a comedy.

ES (*pressing both Mary Ann's hands after a moment's hesitation on his part and hers*): I am delighted to meet you, Mary Ann, if I may. My readers will be most interested in your touching story.

MARY ANN: Readers of what, Elijah?

ES (*visibly startled*): Scribbler, Mr. Elijah Scribbler. I write for Universal News, the most popular journal in the English-speaking world. Or it shall be when its circulation increases. Allow me to offer my sympathy to you for all the vile indignities you must have suffered as a helpless captive.

MARY ANN (*coldly*): You've been misinformed, young man. I am a victim of the vile theft and destruction of my land. Reparations need to be made, but no one has taken up my cause.

ES (*looking confused*): Ah yes, working the land must have been utterly destructive for a girl with tropical sensuality. Mary Ann, I want you to know that my readers have every concern for your suffering, especially the violation of your modesty at the hands of brutish men. Please feel free to unburden yourself completely. Think of me as your friend.

MARY ANN (*suspiciously*): Can you help me get my land back?

ES: You needn't speak in euphemisms, poor girl. How true it is that a female's most precious possession, once stolen, can never be regained. My readers have the greatest respect for outraged maidenhood, and the greatest interest in its degradation. As a warning for others, Mary Ann, would you tell me when your master first tore aside the meager clothing you were forced to wear?

MARY ANN: As a warning, Elijah, I have a proposal for you. If you can provide me with the aid of a lawyer who specializes in real estate cases, at the expense of your newspaper, I will tell you the sordid details of how I lost what was mine.

MR. SCRIBBLER STILL LOOKED BEWILDERED when I bade him adieu, after offering to welcome him back if he returned with legal assistance. Mary Ann stood up and moved steadily toward him until he turned round and bolted into the foyer, from whence he made an undignified escape.

After this episode, Mary Ann decided to seek out the darker inhabitants of London when she accompanied me and Roger on our first visit to my parents since our return. We each accomplished a goal: my joyful reunion with my proud parents and younger siblings, Roger's successful performance as a bridegroom endearing himself to his bride's family, and my dauntless lover's discovery of an assortment of Africans and their descendants.

The second phase of Mary Ann's quest was to find a building which could encompass an office, a stage, and benches for an audience. And thus was launched the Hottentot Theater, headquarters of London's only all-black troupe of traveling players. As directress, Mary Ann styled herself Princess Innay, hereditary ruler of the Elephant Kingdom in deepest Africa.

Together, we adapted my unfinished story about the queen of an island into a musical comedy about an African queen and her army of barely-clad women warriors, every one of them adept in the use of a spear, a dagger or a bow and arrows—although they also loved to dance and sing. Roger's original investment in Mary Ann's company was repaid by the time this first show had completed its first run.

Keeping up with the demand for costumes was a challenge for my own company, but Mary Ann and I worked well together, and several of her actors supported themselves between tours by working for me.

The success of the theater enabled Mary Ann to branch out into ancient Greek and Shakespearean tragedy.

Critics came to the theater to laugh, but they left in tears after watching Mary Ann perform as Medea, the betrayed mother who sacrifices her children. Mary Ann told me privately that she hoped her own mother was invisibly present at every performance. And perhaps she was.

WHERE WAS MY LONG-LOST LUCY? SHE WAS living in Kent with her husband Edward and their little daughter, Margaret Emily. When she first came to Tingley Towers after my arrival as chatelaine, she seemed as pale in her mourning clothes as the heroine of a romance. The black crepe of her ensemble mirrored the glossy black of her hair, now tightly confined and not allowed to flow over her shoulders in girlish ringlets.

Cowardice, I thought, *brings its own punishment.* For a moment, I felt as though she were publicly mourning the freedom of her school days and our youthful *affaire du coeur.*

"Emily," she greeted me. "I'm so glad you've returned from that dreadful war. And I'm so glad you're married to my brother, so we need never be parted again!" She seemed on the verge of tears.

"Lucy," I said, embracing her like a friend. I couldn't force myself to call her by her married name, Mrs. Settleton. "This is Miss Cornford. I'm sure you've heard of her."

"Charmed," said Lucy, extending her hand. Her smile was cool.

Mary Ann seemed genuinely moved by Lucy's appearance. "The feeling is entirely mutual, Mrs. Settleton," she said, "and I'm very sorry for your loss. I'm sure you and Lady Lowerend have so much to say to each other. When you have something to say to me, please call me Mary Ann. Meanwhile, I'll give you both some time alone." Mary Ann gracefully backed away and walked to another part of the garden where she pretended to inspect the rosebushes.

"Lucy," I said, "I hope you're happy and well."

"Yes," she answered. It was apparent she did not want to give me a precise account of her emotional state.

I couldn't help comparing my two women lovers: the wilting English lily and the robust American sunflower. In a fit of spite, I told Lucy, "She isn't my maid, you know."

For an instant, I saw the old fire in her eyes. "Clearly not, Emily," she replied.

Oh, Lucy, I thought. *What did you expect?*

FORTUNATELY, ROGER'S OTHER SIBLINGS were more welcoming than their mother and less troubled than Lucy. His sister Amelia returned from Paris, where she had been studying to be a painter, with her dear friend

Lorraine de la Trompe L'oeil. Amelia introduced the Mademoiselle to everyone she knew as a brilliant portrait-painter whose work could only increase in value over time. Roger and I hired her to paint our wedding portrait.

For this occasion, we both wore the same clothes we had worn to the Palace, and Lorraine faithfully reproduced the texture of the fabric on canvas. She showed us holding hands and smiling intimately at each other, not at the viewer, against the dramatic background of a stormy sea. When the painting was on public display, the painter was widely discussed for her avant-garde approach to a traditional subject.

An illustration of this painting appeared in Universal News, and it caused us to be recognized wherever we went. As Roger's brother Lionel proudly told us, Prince Edward himself observed that the picture of Lord and Lady Lowerend represented the very best sort of modern English marriage, a union which can weather the storms of life.

Fifteen

Postscript

"ARE YOU ABSOLUTELY SURE, DEAREST?" I asked Mary Ann as she pressed an ear to my hard, round belly.

She grinned at me. "Your condition must make you confused, Emily. You asked me two questions and didn't wait for an answer. Anyway, my answer is yes. Yes, I heard a heartbeat. And yes, honey, call me the Devil's own fool if I ever get into the same predicament. You can be fruitful and multiply as much as you like, but I won't let a man of any color plant his seed inside me. I like my body the way it is."

We sat together on the grass in the walled section of the Fruit Garden, enjoying the sun on our naked skin. Birds sang serenades and daisies curtseyed to the breeze.

"Please don't go on tour during my confinement," I begged.

"Now, Emily," my lover chided. "You know we'll all be here, me and our two husbands. Why do you think they're away now? A yacht isn't exactly a ship, but it gives them a little reminder of life at sea before they settle down to become fathers."

The sounds of clashing swords and shouted taunts reached us from the other side of the wall; Mary Ann's actors were rehearsing a battle scene.

I wished I knew how to prepare for my own coming ordeal.

Mary Ann seemed amused by the sight of my swollen breasts, crowned with nipples like brown cherries, and the ivory mound beneath them. I couldn't see the triangle of hair between my thighs because my belly obscured everything below it. Seen from above, it looked as large and spherical as a planet.

Without a word, Mary Ann stood up and lowered herself to the ground so that her back was propped against an apple tree. She pulled me against her, pressing her own firm bubbies against my back and my hair, which now hung almost to my waist. She wrapt her arms round my shoulders and combed my locks with her fingers. "Brave little mother," she teased. "I bet you're not scared at all."

"Giving birth must be like passing beyond the grave," I complained. "No one ever comes back to describe it."

"If it's too much to bear, Emily," she said, "you can ask for chloroform. Besides," she mused, "every time is probably different, just like all our times together."

I hadn't thought of childbed in those terms, but Mary Ann's comparison seemed logical. I turned to face her, and she rewarded me with a deep, lingering kiss.

Melting desire flowed from the pressure of her lips on mine. Despite my condition, it traveled through me like an enchanted stream, and pooled in my unseen center.

Was it sensible for me to crave her touch? Not in the least. "Mary Ann," I confessed, "We ought to stop, but I don't want to. Please be careful."

"Gentle sometimes works best, dear heart," she assured me. "I don't want to harm the child either."

As Mary Ann and I rolled together in the grass for the last time before my little daughter arrived in the world, there was no room inside me for fear or regret.

JEAN ROBERTA is the thin-disguise pen name of an English instructor in a Canadian prairie university, where she is currently co-editing a book of articles based on presentations in a queer faculty speakers series, including her own approach to the notorious 1928 lesbian (or transgendered) novel, *The Well of Loneliness*. An article of hers is due to appear in *From the Coffin to the Classroom, Teaching the Vampire*, in 2014.

She writes more fiction than non-fiction, and over ninety of her erotic stories, including every orientation she can think of, have appeared in print anthologies and two single-author collections.

Her reviews appear in a variety of venues, and she blogs here: www.ohgetagrip.blogspot.com and here: www.erotica-readers.blogspot.com. The twenty-five opinion pieces she wrote for a monthly column, "Sex Is All Metaphors" (on the site of the Erotic Readers and Writers Association, 2008-2010) are available as an e-book, *Sex Is All Metaphors*, here: www.eroticanthology.com/metaphors.htm All profits go to support the National Coalition for Sexual Freedom.